P9-ASF-621

a novel ✷ TRANSLATED FROM THE HEBREW BY ✷ *Bracha Slae*

Jerusalem & New York

BENZION FIRER

The Long Journey Home

FELDHEIM PUBLISHERS

Originally published in Hebrew
as Tahpuchoth haGoral

English version first published 1984
Hardcover edition: ISBN 0-87306-342-2
Paperback edition: ISBN 0-87306-343-0

Phototypeset at the Feldheim Press

Philipp Feldheim Inc.
200 Airport Executive Park
Spring Valley, NY 10977

96 East Broadway
New York, NY 10002

Feldheim Publishers Ltd
POB 6525 / Jerusalem, Israel

Printed in Israel

contents

✱ I ✱ *Shlomo Sharfson*

Eighteen-year-old Shlomo was the apple of his parents' eye and the pride and joy of the Jewish community of Chedalonova. Everyone in the small Polish town had watched this child prodigy grow into a budding young genius, the star pupil of Chedalonova's beloved *Rav*. Although students from all over Poland came to learn Torah with the *Rav* of Chedalonova, Shlomo remained his favorite pupil. The *Rav* had invested much effort in teaching Shlomo, and Shlomo had absorbed almost everything he was taught.

Whenever the *Rav* raised a difficult question for the class and asked for their suggestions before presenting his own solution, Shlomo would be the first to answer. Usually, he was also the last, for his answers generally made any further comments unnecessary. Even when Shlomo's ideas differed from the *Rav*'s, the *Rav* would often defer to him, withholding his own opinion.

Shlomo's father, Reb Kolonymos, was a well-to-do wholesale grain dealer and an honored member of the local Jewish community. His mother, Bathsheva, was well known and respected as a diligent housewife who also found time to devote herself to acts of kindness and charity. Shlomo had a brother David, who was ten years younger than he was, and a sister Sarah, who was two years younger than David.

Most of Shlomo's day was spent in the *Beith Midrash*. He would occupy himself with reviewing yesterday's lesson and preparing for tomorrow's. Shlomo was the envy, not only of his friends in the *Beith Midrash*, but also of their parents. It is natural for someone so gifted to arouse some jealousy, but this was a positive kind of envy, since it was "for the sake of the Torah." Shlomo's friends tried to imitate him and devoted themselves to studying, each according to his own abilities. Even their parents held Shlomo up as an example.

Looking at Shlomo as he sat in the *Beith Midrash*, you would not have guessed his thoughts. You could see his eyes moving across the small print in the open book before him, but you could not see his heart, and sometimes, his heart was elsewhere. Sometimes even his eyes, though glued to his *gemara*, were in reality seeing things that were far away. For Shlomo had seen things in the world around him that had turned his thoughts away from the *Beith Midrash*.

He was not really to blame, for he was born in the stormy era immediately after World War I. Large numbers of soldiers never returned home from that war, and many families had been utterly wiped out. The spiritual damage, brought by the new winds to towns even as small as Chedalonova, was even more devastating. New, "modern" philosophies began to compete with the *gemara*. It was not unusual for a young man to close his *gemara* for good and to leave the *Beith Midrash* without even kissing the *mezuzah*. And of those who remained, many remained in body only.

These new philosophies had one thing in common. They all attempted to right some wrong. Some came to reform the entire world, and others merely attempted to reform the Jewish people. Some emphasized the equality of all men in the world, while others emphasized the equality of Jews and non-Jews. One aimed to provide every human being with food and clothing, while another wished to win freedom and equality for Jews among the nations. And one demanded a homeland for the Jews, just like that of all the other nations.

Each of these factions opened its own clubhouse in Chedalonova. Those who strove for equality among all human beings opened a club for Jews and non-Jews together, while those who worried primarily about the Jews opened clubs for Jews only.

The group that strove for a Jewish homeland was called Hechalutz. Hechalutz did not believe, as their friends in the Bund did, that Jews could ever achieve equality in the Diaspora. But they did believe that if the Jews had their own homeland, they would gain the honor and respect of the non-Jewish world. They believed that anti-Semitism was the natural result of the fact that Jews had been "uninvited guests" in other peoples' countries. This understandable hatred of Jews had been fanned by the fact that Jews had traditionally turned to commerce instead of to constructive professions such as farming. Lending money was unjust; it was neither a necessary nor an honorable profession. Were Jews to work their own land, anti-Semitism would soon disappear.

The Bund also disapproved of commercial professions, but they believed that the country in which each person, Jew or non-Jew, was born, was his rightful homeland. Although most of the Gentile world still opposed the idea of equal rights for Jews, the Jews would nonetheless be able to achieve equality if only they cooperated with those few Gentiles who did seek justice in the world.

The Bund had two flags, neither of which was exclusively their own. One was red and white—the Polish national flag—and one was all red—the international laborer's flag. Hechalutz had its own special flag—blue and white—alongside the red, proletariat flag. Although none of the *chalutzim* lived by the sweat of his brow as yet, they saw themselves as workers of the future. They were still being supported by their parents, but soon they would be farmers in Eretz Yisrael. Hechalutz members also had their own uniform—blue pants and white shirt. Every year on the first of May they would march together with members of the Bund and non-Jewish idealists, waving the red flag and singing Polish songs. But on the twentieth of *Tammuz* they would march down the street in their blue and white uniforms, waving their own blue and white flag and singing Hebrew songs.

The boys who sat and learned in the *Beith Midrash* had nothing to do with either group. Nevertheless, on the twentieth of *Tammuz* a few boys could be seen leaving their *gemaroth* for a minute and going to the doorstep of the *Beith Midrash* to watch Hechalutz's parade go by and to listen to their songs, even though the Hebrew of the *chalutzim* sounded different from the Hebrew of the *Beith Midrash* and they could not always understand it. One of those who got up to watch the parade was Shlomo.

Why would someone like Shlomo, who was so engrossed in learning Torah, turn to these idle pursuits? Heaven forbid that he be caught in the net of such a godless group. When the *Rav* was told that Shlomo had left his *gemara* to watch the parade, he sighed and said, "The Torah grants protection. It will save him from sin." Nevertheless, it was clear that the *Rav* was deeply disturbed.

✱ 2 ✱ *Shlomo the Woodchopper*

The *chalutzim* had to train themselves to do manual labor. In Eretz Yisrael they would be farmers and raise their own crops, so it was essential for them to learn how to work. Their main interest was in farming, but unfortunately, there was no Jewish land in Chedalonova for them to farm. The Jewish houses were all built around the marketplace, one on top of the other, with the main street in front of them and the market behind. There was not enough room to stick a needle between one house and the next. Every inch of land was covered with buildings.

Only one of the *chalutzim* had the good fortune to live a bit farther away from the marketplace. He had a small yard where he planted green onions and garlic and radishes. He watered and weeded them faithfully, training himself to be a farmer.

The *chalutzim* who had no opportunity to do farming did any sort of manual labor they could find, but in the summertime there was hardly any work. Once in a great while Reb Kolonymos would give them a few sacks of grain to carry. All summer they waited for the fall, their best season of the year, for in the fall each household was busy storing up woodpiles to fuel the furnaces in the winter. The villagers would bring sawed-off tree branches from the forest. These had to be split into pieces that would fit into the furnaces. This was a job for strong men and sharp hatchets. Reb Kolonymos, who had a large house and many rooms to heat, provided them with employment for many days.

Sometimes uncut branches several feet long would be brought to the market. Then two *chalutzim* would stand opposite each other, the branch on a plank between them, until they managed to saw it in half. After they had split the branch into logs, they would split the logs into thin planks of the required size. Some of the *chalutzim* were the sons of well-to-do families who could afford to hire workers to split logs. In that case each *chalutz* would work for his friend's father. Splitting logs for your own father was not considered working.

A few of Chedalonova's Jews made a point of employing only non-Jews, thereby conveying their opposition to the *chalutzim*. But on the whole, the *chalutzim* were not taken very seriously. Few people believed that youths from good families would exchange the comforts of home for a farmer's life in Eretz Yisrael. Perhaps young people from poor families would do so, but not those from wealthy homes. One such youth had already gone to Eretz Yisrael and come back home to his family in Chedalonova. He claimed that the doctors there had sent him home, but no one believed that that was the whole truth.

The sight of *chalutzim* splitting wood was no longer a novelty in Chedalonova, and it drew no special attention.

People were too involved in their own affairs to stand around watching them. Each shop owner was busy waiting for customers to buy his food, clothing, or dry goods, and those shop owners who had competitors nearby were doubly busy, as they also had to keep track of how much business, if any, the competing stores were doing.

But not only the rich needed logs for heating their houses in the winter. If anything, the poor needed them more, for the rich had money to warm their hearts, as well as sufficient food and clothing. With a full stomach and warm clothing one is not so cold. Wood in the winter was much more important to the poor, who had no money and little food and clothing. They could not buy enough wood in the fall for the entire winter; a few weeks' worth of wood was the most they could afford. After that, they would look to charity, a quality never lacking among Jews. A few members of the community had accepted the responsibility for this *mitzvah*. They would make the rounds of the stores and collect money to buy wood for the poor. Among those who made the rounds was Shlomo's mother, Bathsheva.

The *chalutzim* also had a share in this *mitzvah*. They gave not money, but time. They would split cheap, uncut branches into logs, and then chop them into pieces. For this work they accepted no remuneration. First of all, they were not really in need of money—the purpose of their work was to acquire expertise and experience. Yankel the Miser had once jokingly remarked that he would hire the *chalutzim* only if *they* paid *him*, as it was he who was doing them a favor. If the *chalutzim* took money from the rich, it was only to show their disapproval of the wealthy and to make them a few pennies poorer. On the other hand, the *chalutzim* felt a special sympathy for the poor and wanted to help them.

Early one cold winter morning, the shopkeepers were standing in their empty stores. They hopped from one foot to the other to keep from freezing, as they warmed their hands around small cooking pots on the stoves. The marketplace was empty. It had snowed all night long and the thick layer of snow made walking difficult.

Two young men appeared and began splitting logs in front of the basement apartment of Senderil the Shoemaker. One of them was Shlomo Sharfson. At first, the shopkeepers who noticed him were so surprised that no one moved, but in a few minutes people started to appear from all directions. Men, women and children came to see Shlomo Sharfson, out of the *Beith Midrash*, chopping wood. As the news spread, boys even ran out of *cheder* to watch him. Shlomo, for his part, continued chopping wood in the center of the ever growing circle of onlookers. To some, this was a funny sight—to others, a sad one. Shlomo stood there splitting logs in his long black coat without even lowering his eyes, showing no visible signs of embarrassment or shame at all the attention. He looked straight into the eyes of all those surrounding him, smiling his usual good-natured smile.

But no one could stand the fierce cold for long. Little by little, the bystanders left, leaving Shlomo and his friend to their work.

Like people the world over, some of the Jews of Chedalonova were good-hearted and shared their friends' distress, while others took pleasure in their neighbors' downfall. Here, too, there were those who rejoiced at Reb

Kolonymos' misfortune, and wished to have a closer look. Reb Kolonymos' shop, with its transparent glass doors, was in the center of the market. Some evil-hearted Jews "happened" to pass by and look inside. When they saw that the store was empty and locked, they exchanged knowing grins as if to say, "We know why!"

Those who sympathized with Reb Kolonymos went to consult the *Rav*. One of them said to him, "Those branches that Shlomo was sawing for Senderil were bought from charity money collected that very morning by Shlomo's own mother. Rabbi Chanina ben Dosa already asked, 'Is it possible for the deeds of a righteous person to cause his descendants to falter and stumble?' "

The *Rav* looked straight at his questioners and answered, "Shlomo has not faltered. On the contrary, he is bringing his mother's act of charity to completion."

"But," objected the questioner, "Shlomo's actions have brought him into the company of freethinkers. They will eventually cause him to stop observing the Torah and the *mitzvoth*."

"The Torah will protect him," countered the *Rav*. "The Torah that Shlomo is learning will save him from sin."

"Excuse me," objected the questioner again, "the *Rav* said 'the Torah that Shlomo is learning'. Perhaps it would be more correct to say 'the Torah that Shlomo has learned until now.' The freethinking *chalutzim* do not usually learn Torah." The *Rav* did not answer.

When the men left the *Rav's* apartment they said to each other, "Love is blind. The *Rav* cannot accept the truth about his beloved pupil Shlomo."

Reb Kolonymos entered the *Rav*'s house as they were leaving. Perhaps the *Rav* changed his mind somewhat about Shlomo after hearing what Reb Kolonymos had to say, but since there were no witnesses to the conversation, the outcome is a matter of pure speculation.

✳ 3 ✳ *Shlomo in Public and in Private*

From the very day Shlomo joined the Moadon Hechalutz—the pioneer's meeting house—his attitude toward certain *mitzvoth* underwent a subtle change. He no longer kept a basin and a cup of water near his bed to wash his hands each morning upon arising. He no longer got up so early in the morning, and more than once, he was late for prayers. Nor did he attend the *Rav*'s Talmud lessons any more. He missed going to the class very much, but he did not want to compromise his teacher. He was afraid of the gossip, of the people who might accuse the *Rav* of not following the Talmudic dictum, "One who teaches an unworthy pupil may be compared to an idol worshiper" (*Chulin* 133). Shlomo knew that he had been branded an errant son. Public opinion was against him, and if the *Rav* did not drive him away, people would speak evil of the *Rav*. Shlomo did not want to cause any injury whatsoever to his teacher, so he sat at home and no longer frequented the *Beith Midrash*.

His evenings were spent at the Moadon. There too, he was considered an alien, even though no one knew that he still prayed three times a day, put on *tefillin* daily, and kept Shabbath. These were things he did privately, at home. But

Shlomo betrayed himself whenever a discussion took place in the Moadon.

Everyone agreed that each nation must have its own country, but how the country should function was still a matter for debate. However, they all disapproved of the Jews of Chedalonova. They were sure that an independent Jewish people in its own homeland would be different from these Jews. The new generation in Eretz Yisrael would be Jews without Shabbath, without synagogues, without *tallith* and *tefillin* and the laws of *kashruth*; in short, without anything connecting them to the Jewish religion.

But Shlomo had other ideas. He didn't accept what everyone else seemed to think was perfectly clear. Once, in the heat of a spirited argument between Shlomo and his friends, Peretz jumped up and exclaimed, "Shlomo, how long are you going to straddle both sides of the fence? You must take your choice: either Torah or Eretz Yisrael!"

"No," answered Shlomo. "The two are indivisible. The Torah has commanded every Jewish person to live in Eretz Yisrael, not in Chedalonova. Therefore, *chalutzim* must not divorce themselves from the Torah. It supports and helps them."

But Peretz would not give in. "Someone with so many *mitzvoth* on his mind cannot concentrate on the *mitzvah* of Eretz Yisrael. Give up worrying about the other *mitzvoth* so you can concentrate on settling Eretz Yisrael!"

"You needn't worry," replied Shlomo, "Eretz Yisrael is not just one of the *mitzvoth*. It is a central *mitzvah*, and the *Geulah*, the Redemption, is a vital part of our prayers. It cannot be pushed aside or forgotten."

"Then why do your friends in the *Beith Midrash* oppose us? Why don't they also join the Moadon and strive to go to Eretz Yisrael? Apparently they don't agree with you either. No one seems to agree with you—neither they nor we. You must make your choice," concluded Peretz.

"I don't know why the other students in the *Beith Midrash* don't participate in the efforts to build up Eretz Yisrael, but I do know that my opinion is not my own invention. It is the opinion of the Torah. Any Jew who goes to Eretz Yisrael is fulfilling a commandment," declared Shlomo.

The *chalutzim* could not judge whether Shlomo's opinions were valid or not. They only knew that they could not accept them. Shlomo bothered them. They could not win an argument with him as he always had an answer to their questions and a question for their answers. And he always won. "It's no wonder," they explained to themselves, "after all those years he spent in the *Beith Midrash* sharpening his mind."

There were several girls in the Moadon. These *chalutzoth*, however, had no opportunity to gain any practical experience in pioneering work in Chedalonova. Woodchopping was not for them. Of course, all members of the Moadon opposed discrimination based upon sex. Men and women should be completely equal in their rights and duties, including work opportunities. This was fine in theory, but in practice, it was very difficult for the girls to saw logs or chop wood. Instead, they decorated the Moadon. They stretched strips of blue and white ribbon across the ceiling and hung pictures of labor Zionist leaders on the walls.

One of the *chalutzoth*, Zissel Blitz, was a graduate of the Polish gymnasium in Cracow. Zissel had noticed Shlomo from the very first day he appeared in the Moadon, although he had not so much as glanced her way. Shlomo was not used to being in mixed company, and did not pay any attention to the girls. Zissel had listened to the argument between Shlomo and Peretz and had been deeply impressed. Not that she always agreed with Shlomo, but she admired him and the confident, polished presentation of his ideas.

While she herself did not debate with Shlomo, Zissel often tried to draw her friends into an argument with him. She herself lacked the ideological background to become involved in these discussions, but she was content to sit back and listen to Shlomo argue with the others. Only once had Zissel asked for permission to speak in the Moadon. At that time she had turned to Shlomo and asked, "Shlomo, as a representative of the *Beith Midrash*, how do you justify the traditional discrimination against women?"

While Zissel was speaking, Shlomo had looked intently at his shoes. Now that she had finished, he continued to look down, but he smiled as he answered, "According to the Torah, men and women are equally liable to punishment for all infractions of the Torah."

Zissel laughed and said, "Very nice. Women deserve equal punishment but not equal rights."

Shlomo stopped smiling and became serious.

"In a household where two opinions are of equal weight, there can be no unity. A Jewish home must be unified, not divided. The man represents the head of the house and the woman represents the heart. It is proper to accord the head priority over the heart, for only the brain is capable of evaluating and controlling a person's actions. Emotions are unstable and can change constantly. They should be controlled by the brain; not vice versa."

It was hard to tell whether Shlomo's answer satisfied or convinced Zissel; all one could say was that she listened to him intently. But perhaps she was more interested in the way Shlomo spoke than in the actual content of his words.

It is impossible to guess what the outcome of these debates would have been, or how long they would have gone on, had not fate removed Shlomo from the Moadon. No, he did not return to the *Beith Midrash*; he left Chedalonova completely. At that time, Eretz Yisrael was under the rule of the British Mandate. In order to prevent the growth of the Jewish population in the country, the British severely limited immigration. Only those lucky enough to hold a British certificate were allowed to enter. These certificates were immigration permits, issued by the British mandatory government and distributed by the Jewish Agency to Jewish communities throughout the world, according to the size of the local Jewish population.

That year, Chedalonova was awarded only two certificates. The members of the Moadon were called upon to decide who would be given the opportunity to settle in Eretz Yisrael. Peretz suggested that one certificate be given to Shlomo, but he met much opposition. Shlomo was only a newcomer; there were veteran *chalutzim* who had been waiting for a certificate for a long time.

"Nevertheless," declared Peretz, "we must send Shlomo to Eretz Yisrael as quickly as possible. He is not really one of us, and as long as he remains in Chedalonova, there is a chance that he may return to the *Beith Midrash*. Once he is in Eretz Yisrael, he will go to a *kibbutz*. There he will forget the *Beith Midrash* of Chedalonova and become a true *chalutz*.

"We must also consider the example Shlomo will set for his friends in the *Beith Midrash*. He will be the first to leave, and many others are likely to follow in his footsteps. Not all of them are as stubborn as he, nor have they learned as much Torah. With Shlomo in Eretz Yisrael, it will be easier for us to influence them." Peretz's speech was highly convincing, and his friends agreed to grant Shlomo one of the certificates.

In keeping with the rule that the sexes be treated equally, the second certificate was to be allotted to a girl. Here, too, Peretz spoke up. "The second certificate must go to Zissel Blitz. The trip to Eretz Yisrael is long. It takes weeks, or even months. It will give Shlomo an opportunity to influence his traveling companion in ways we might not approve of. Zissel is the only girl who would not be susceptible to Shlomo's influence because of her utter lack of any Jewish background. Her father is an assimilated Polish lawyer and she received a strictly Polish education. Shlomo cannot influence her, as she has no Jewish memories for him to awaken. No other girl in Chedalonova comes from such an assimilated family."

Once again, Peretz made his point, and Zissel received the second certificate.

Truth to tell, Shlomo's religious beliefs had weakened recently, along with his practical adherence to the *mitzvoth*. A few days before, he had forgotten to put on his *tefillin* in the morning, and the previous Shabbath he had absent-mindedly walked outside with a handkerchief in his pocket.

Nevertheless, he would not allow himself to be bested in the debates in the Moadon.

Man is a perverse animal. Shlomo had devoted many years of his life to studying Torah, and this Torah had become his own personal possession. Shlomo would not allow Peretz, who had never studied the Torah, to ridicule it or take it away from him. On the other hand, Shlomo felt that he himself could afford to neglect the Torah a bit, since it was his own "property." But he would protect it from any damage by others.

Perhaps, had Peretz accepted part of Shlomo's opinions on the centrality of the Torah to Eretz Yisrael, Shlomo might also have accepted part of Peretz's views about rebuilding a new and different Jewish people. However, since Peretz, not having studied psychology, said exactly what he thought, Shlomo felt called upon to defend his stand vigorously and at all costs.

In short, none of the girls of Chedalonova were in danger of being lured back to the Torah by Shlomo, since he himself was no longer as devout as he had once been. But because Peretz was ignorant of this fact, Zissel received the second certificate.

∗ 4 ∗ *On the Way to Eretz Yisrael*

The following evening, when Shlomo walked into the Moadon, he was greeted with cries of "*Mazal tov*!" He looked around uncomprehendingly. Peretz walked over to him and held out a folded piece of paper.

"You're a lucky fellow!" he said. "Here it is!"

"Here is what?" asked Shlomo.

"You have been awarded a certificate!" answered Peretz, opening the paper and displaying it for all to see.

Shlomo was stunned. He didn't know whether to rejoice or to refuse the honor. He covered his confusion with a smile and simply said, "Thank you."

Later, when his friends had turned their attention to other matters, Shlomo began to examine his own feelings.

Evidently the townspeople were right. These spoiled children did not readily exchange their comfortable homes for a life of hard labor in Eretz Yisrael and so they gave the prized certificates away to newcomers like himself. Words were cheap, but Shlomo would prove to them that he, at least, practiced what he preached. But he could not rejoice in his decision. The *Beith Midrash* in Chedalonova was still the center of his world and leaving it would be painful.

After a while, he went home to break the news to his parents. His father let out a deep sigh. Until now, he had been hoping that the Moadon was a passing fancy. He had hoped that one day Shlomo would sober up and return to the *Beith Midrash*. If Shlomo joined the *chalutzim* in Eretz Yisrael he might never set foot in a *Beith Midrash* again.

"What will you do?" Kolonymos asked his son.

"If I have been awarded a certificate, then I must go to Eretz Yisrael," answered Shlomo.

"Can't you thank them for their goodwill and return the certificate? There are many others who would be only too happy to take your place."

"I don't want people to say that an observant Jew does not practice what he preaches. That would be a disgrace—a *chillul haShem*," countered Shlomo.

"Perhaps there is still hope for him," thought Kolonymos. "He still considers himself a *ben Torah* who doesn't want to cause any *chillul haShem*!"

Kolonymos was silent. The *Rav* had advised him not to scold Shlomo or argue with him as Shlomo was stubborn and would not give in easily. Harsh words might drive him away from them forever. But now, when it seemed that Shlomo was leaving them anyway, perhaps the time had come to speak frankly and to tell him how much sorrow and shame he was causing his family by joining a group of nonbelieving, non-observant Jews.

But on second thought, Kolonymos decided no, the *Rav*'s advice still held. The spirit of folly that had entered Shlomo in Chedalonova might leave him in Eretz Yisrael.

Bathsheva, seeing that her husband had given Shlomo his

tacit assent, began to grieve. "Shlomoleh, my son, what will we do without you? The house will be empty. How can you do such a cruel thing to your father and mother?"

Shlomo answered haltingly, "I cannot put the *Beith Midrash* to shame. People will say, 'Look at him—the *ben Torah*! He talked a lot about the importance of *aliyah* to Eretz Yisrael, but when he was given the chance, he refused. All talk and no action, that's what they are in the *Beith Midrash*!' There could be no *chillul haShem* greater than that." Hearing Shlomo mention *chillul haShem* again, Bathsheva grew silent. She understood and accepted his words.

When Zissel received her certificate, the news came as a shock to her, too. At first she refused the honor, claiming that she was a new member of Hechalutz, and she had much to learn before she could become a pioneer in Eretz Yisrael. Peretz waited for Zissel to finish speaking, and then he smiled and said, "Shlomo Sharfson was also awarded a certificate." Zissel blushed, and lowering her eyes, she examined the certificate again.

At home, Zissel's announcement was met with a flat refusal. Her father, Edmond Blitz, claimed that Poland was their homeland. It was true that some Poles were anti-Semitic and even dared to use physical violence against Jews. As a lawyer he had recently brought two such Poles to trial. But the Jews were at fault. They angered the Poles by claiming that Palestine rather than Poland was their homeland. The Poles would not hate Jews who were loyal Polish patriots. Mr. Blitz had opposed Zissel's membership in the Moadon from the very beginning. He had permitted her to go because she had no other friends in Chedalonova. Very few Polish girls attended the gymnasium, and the girls from the Jewish gymnasium all belonged to the Moadon. But *aliyah* to Israel was an altogether different matter. It was absolutely unthinkable.

In his consternation, poor Edmond completely forgot to ask who else had received certificates. It was Rozeshka, Zissel's mother, who heard in the market that Reb Kolonymos Sharfson's son had received the second certificate. "What a disgrace—to go with a Talmudist from the *Beith Midrash*!" wailed Rozeshka.

"A Talmudist? What Talmudist?" asked Edmond.

"The boy with the long black coat who split logs for Senderil the Shoemaker—that's who she's going with!" cried Rozeshka.

That was the last straw. Calling her by her Polish name as befit a member of their family, Zissel's father decreed, "Zushka, I absolutely forbid you to take part in this!"

Now Zissel was an only child who knew her own power. There was nothing she could not get if she was only stubborn enough. She let her parents vent all their frustration and anger, knowing full well that, in the end, she would get her own way. And she was right.

You may indeed ask how Zissel's parents—with no ties to their fellow Jews or to Eretz Yisrael—could give in. How could they allow their only daughter to forsake them and leave Poland to live in a foreign land? Their reasoning was that when Zissel had experienced hunger and hard life in the new country, she would quickly return. Her own experience would prove to her that her place was in Poland.

The date was set for Shlomo and Zissel's departure. The

route was well known: a train would take them from Chedalonova to Cracow, the meeting place for *olim* from Galicia. From Cracow they would take another train to Vienna, then on to Trieste, and from there they would set sail for Haifa.

The *chalutzim* celebrated the day of their departure as if it were a holiday. Dressed in blue and white, they accompanied Shlomo and Zissel from the Moadon to the train station, singing all the way. Edmond and Rozeshka Blitz had come by themselves and were already waiting at the station. They had not wanted to accompany the *chalutzim*, who were much too Jewish for them. They had never dreamed that such a tragedy would befall their family. When Zissel finally arrived at the station and caught sight of her parents, her heart sank. Their anguish was so great that she wondered if she was doing the right thing. Her friends acted as though she were a bride being led to the wedding canopy, but her parents looked as though they were at her funeral. Zissel ran over to her parents, kissed them hard and whispered something that was lost in all the noise. Perhaps she asked their forgiveness and promised to write. Their eyes were full of tears. They prayed that none of their Polish friends were present to witness their disgrace.

Reb Kolonymos and Bathsheva, together with Sarah and David, stood at the other end of the station, searching for their son Shlomo among the crowd. They had already taken their leave of him at home before he left for the Moadon. Good-byes such as these were not public affairs. Shlomo left his friends for a minute and went over to his family. They said a simple good-bye once again, nodding their heads to one another. The adults in Reb Kolonymos' family did not kiss in public. When the engine began to shriek, Shlomo shook his father's hand, nodded to his mother, and said "*Shalom.*" He kissed little Sarah and David again and reminded them to be good. Then he quickly returned to his friends. Zissel left her parents and ran toward the group from the opposite direction. People jostled each other as they got off and on the train. Shlomo and Zissel were lost in the crowd as they, too, pushed their way toward the train. Only the group of *chalutzim* stood out, singing their Hebrew songs, causing Poles to spit and curse, "Let the damn Jews go to Palestine."

✷ 5 ✷ *A Meeting in the Train*

Once aboard the train, Shlomo and Zissel hurried to the window for a last glimpse of their friends and families. The locomotive let out a shriek and the train started on its way. Everyone waved his handkerchief and shouted "*Shalom*" until the train pulled out of the station.

Shlomo and Zissel left the window and turned toward the train's passengers. Just then several young people approached them, and welcomed them aboard. Shlomo and Zissel returned the greeting with a blank stare until the youths explained that they, too, were on their way to Eretz Yisrael. Shmuel and Sheindel were from Nachrovah and Aharon and Elka were from Temyonovah. They were members of Hashomer Hatzair, not of Hechalutz. Shlomo had never before heard of Hashomer Hatzair. As a newcomer to the Moadon—straight from the *Beith Midrash*—he had thought that everyone who wanted to live in Eretz Yisrael was a *chalutz* and that there were no differences of opinion among *chalutzim*.

The six boys and girls sat down in one corner of the coach and began to talk.

"Could you explain exactly what Hashomer Hatzair is?" asked Shlomo.

"Hashomer Hatzair emphasizes self-improvement and social reform," answered Aharon. "If every individual relinquishes his privacy and his personal property in order to share a communal life in which no one owns anything of his own and all are equal, then we will have cured all of the world's ills."

"But you could do that in Poland," said Shlomo. "Why are you going to Eretz Yisrael?"

"Because we are also Zionists," replied Shmuel, "but we emphasize social equality. We are going to Eretz Yisrael to establish a communal life. For us, Eretz Yisrael without social reform has no value. We want to realize in Eretz Yisrael what other idealistic nations will realize in their own homelands. Actually, we feel much closer to fellow idealists who are not Jewish, than to Jews who go to Eretz Yisrael simply out of fear of the gentiles. For us, Eretz Yisrael is the means to an end, not the end itself. Our real goal is social reform, and if we had to choose, we would prefer social reform in the diaspora over life in Eretz Yisrael without reform."

Shmuel's speech shocked Shlomo. He had always thought that those who waved the blue and white flag were unconditionally committed to Eretz Yisrael. Now he had learned that for at least one sector, social reform rather than Eretz Yisrael was the primary goal. But Shlomo had never been an easy person to convince, and he stuck to his own opinion now, too.

"Why go to all the trouble of settling in Eretz Yisrael if social reform is possible in Poland? Eretz Yisrael itself is my ideal, and fellow Jews who share this feeling are closer to me than any non-Jew, idealistic as he may be."

"What about religion?" asked Elka. "Whom do you prefer—a 'synagogue Jew' or an enlightened, tolerant non-Jew?"

"From my experience," insisted Shlomo, "the synagogue Jews are devoted heart and soul to Eretz Yisrael, even if they do oppose the *chalutzim*. On the other hand, I do not trust non-Jews, enlightened or tolerant though they may be. Their tolerance is just a mask, and their equality a ruse."

After a short pause, Shlomo added, "I, too, could be called a synagogue Jew. I have learned much Torah in the *Beith Midrash*, including the saying of our sages, 'It is an incontrovertible law that Esau hates Jacob.' "

"I'm surprised that you are a member of Hechalutz," Sheindel replied. "You would fit in much better in Betar."

Shlomo knew that Sheindel was right, but there had been no branch of Betar in Chedalonova. Now that he was going to Eretz Yisrael as a representative of Hechalutz, he had to rationalize his choice somehow. To Sheindel he replied, "I belong in Hechalutz because I believe in pioneering action."

Zissel had not taken part in the debate as she was not certain of her own opinions. Nevertheless, she had followed the argument closely and she knew that she agreed with Shlomo only partially. She was pleased that equality was not his ideal in life. She, too, did not think that the prime goal of society was to achieve equality between Senderil the Shoemaker and her father, the lawyer. On the other hand, she disliked Shlomo's hatred of non-Jews.

For the *chalutzim* who were engrossed in the discussion, time flew by, but for Zissel, the hours seemed to crawl. While studying in the gymnasium she had often taken the train to Cracow and she knew the route well. Zissel got up and walked over to the window to watch the farmers working in their fields. It was a beautiful summer day and the landscape unfolded before her eyes like a patchwork quilt—large squares of grain and smaller squares of vegetables—each a different color. As Zissel gazed at the beautiful scenery, she began to doubt herself. No matter how she tried, she was not really at ease with these Jewish youths who felt themselves so foreign to Poland, and who thought only of Eretz Yisrael. They felt that their having been born in Poland was pure chance and had no meaning. Perhaps her father was right. Perhaps she really belonged back with her friends from the Polish gymnasium.

Not perhaps. Certainly. She knew that the real reason for her acceptance of the certificate was her attraction to Shlomo, but Shlomo hardly paid any attention to her. She wondered how he would have behaved had they been traveling without the group. Would he have bothered to talk to her at all? She could not forget how he had avoided looking at her when she had turned to him in the Moadon and asked him about discrimination against women.

Just then Zissel heard her name. She turned around and saw that the group was eating. Shlomo, a small suitcase on his lap and a piece of cake in his hand, said to her, " 'Without bread, there can be no Torah.' "

Zissel's doubts suddenly vanished and she beamed at Shlomo, "Thank you." Returning to her place in the circle, she took her share of the cake and said, "I, too, have a cake in my suitcase. Next time we will eat my mother's cake."

"We are already a commune," said Aharon, "sharing whatever we have."

"We're only six members now," added Shmuel, "but in another three hours the commune will grow larger and richer. In Cracow we will join a large group. The food we all own should last us for a few days."

But even as they spoke of communes and shared their food, there was a certain feeling of estrangement from Shlomo. They tried to ignore it or drive it away, but it persisted. When they finished eating, they all became quiet and withdrawn. The stormy debate had tired them out. One leaned against the wall and tried to take a nap. Another was engrossed in his own private world. A third went to look out the window and a fourth sat there, just plain bored.

Zissel, however, felt better. Her former doubts melted away. She had the feeling that, somehow, her future would be tied to Shlomo's.

A deafening whistle announced that they were rapidly approaching the familiar glass-roofed platforms of the Cracow train station. Straightening her dress, Zissel turned around and saw her friends taking their suitcases and knapsacks and preparing to get off the train. Suitcase in hand, she took her place among the group.

* 6 * *Cracow*

In Cracow, the six youths found the Jewish Agency hostel a teeming beehive. Its large hall was lined with tables and benches. Piles of suitcases and knapsacks of all shapes and sizes were stuffed between the walls and the benches. In the center of the room were groups of young people. Some were idling the time away with gossip, others with jokes. Here and there someone was reading a newspaper or writing in a notebook. Some had already met on the train and were continuing the conversations they had begun during the trip. Although the first groups had arrived two or three days earlier, they had not yet all met. When all the certificate holders arrived, the Jewish Agency would send them all to Vienna.

The arrival of the six newcomers caused everyone to stop and see if these were familiar faces. Seeing that they were strangers, they all returned to their conversations. The newcomers found space for their suitcases and looked around the room. They, too, searched for familiar faces, but not finding any, they remained silent, seating themselves on benches to rest from the trip.

The time was late afternoon. The sun emblazened the sky with brilliant colors. It was the kind of sunset that inspires poets. Shlomo was no poet, but as he looked at the sunset, a verse from Psalms burst from his lips: " 'The heavens declare the glory of God and His works are told of by the firmament.' "

"What did you say?" asked Zissel.

"I said, 'Lift up your eyes to the heavens and see Who has created all these,' " answered Shlomo, indicating the sunset while he quoted from Isaiah.

"Whom were you talking to?" asked Zissel.

"To everyone here."

"But no one was listening."

"Even if they had heard me they would not have understood."

"If so, then whom were you talking to?" persisted Zissel.

"I suppose I was talking to myself," muttered Shlomo.

"You were talking to me, too. I understood what you said," Zissel tried to comfort him.

Shlomo laughed. "You will end up a *rebbetzin* yet and you will cause your father much suffering."

"There could be worse tragedies," laughed Zissel.

After a while, some of the *chalutzim* began to set the tables with trays of bread and butter, cheese and radishes. Others brought cups of steaming coffee, and everyone was called to supper. The invitation met with an immediate response by the hungry pioneers. When they finished eating and ended the discussions begun before supper, it was time to go to sleep. The young men remained in the dining hall. They covered the floor with straw mattresses and each traveler received two sheets—one to cover the mattress and one to cover himself. The young women slept in another room, but they, too, were pioneers and were treated accordingly. They, too, slept on sheets and straw mattresses.

Shlomo was tired. The second he put his head down on the mattress he fell asleep. But after an hour or two he awoke. He suddenly recalled that he had neither recited the afternoon *mincha* and evening *maariv* prayers, nor had he said the *Shema* before retiring. This reminded him that he had not recited the Grace after Meals either, nor had he washed his hands or recited the blessing before eating. The blessings over food were lost forever, but he could still make up the evening prayers that he had forgotten. He could get up now and pray. And he could recite the *Shema* all night long. Nevertheless, he did not get up. He didn't know the reason why, but he did know that he remained lying in his straw bed.

Shlomo thought to himself, "There must be two Shlomos inside of me: one who scolds for not getting up to pray, and the other who holds me back from praying. I know the Shlomo who is scolding me, but where did the other Shlomo come from?"

The "other Shlomo" was, of course, from the Moadon. When Shlomo left the *Beith Midrash* and entered the world of the Moadon, the other Shlomo made his appearance. Now both halves of Shlomo were fighting, not letting him sleep. One urged him to get up—the other to lie down. Between the two, he lost a good night's sleep. When the Angel of Sleep saw Shlomo's suffering he took pity on him and made him drowsy. Nevertheless, Shlomo remained half asleep and half awake. Not even the good angel could help him sleep peacefully that night.

The next morning Shlomo was very tired. The boys collected the mattresses and stacked them outside so the room could serve as a dining hall again. Everyone washed up, polished his shoes or sewed a button on a shirt, and soon all were ready for breakfast.

As Zissel walked into the dining hall, she searched for Shlomo, and when she found him, she came over.

"Good morning," he said.

"Good morning to you," said Zissel. "How did you sleep?"

"I would not be so tired now if I had slept at night," grumbled Shlomo.

"And why didn't you sleep?"

"It's hard to sleep in a new place."

"I slept very well."

"Well, not everyone is so lucky. Enjoy your good fortune."

Seeing that Shlomo was in a bad mood, Zissel changed the subject. "After breakfast, let's go for a walk. Cracow is a beautiful city and I can show you some things that will help you forget your fatigue."

The *chalutzim* had not expected the Jewish Agency to feed them royally and the simple breakfast was identical with their supper. It did not take long to finish eating and leave the table.

Shlomo did not eat at all. He was still disturbed by the night's struggle. Zissel noticed his lack of appetite and began to think that perhaps he was ill. As they left the table, she again invited him to go for a walk.

"Where shall we go?" he asked.

"Let's go out of the Jewish ghetto and walk south toward Vavel," suggested Zissel.

"What can we see there?"

"The graves of Polish royalty."

"I am not interested in Polish royalty," said Shlomo, "Poland is not my homeland. The Poles hate us."

But Zissel persisted, "The famous poet Adam Mitchkevitz is also buried there. I will recite some of his poetry to you. Some say that he was of Jewish descent and was a friend of the Jews."

"What good will it do to hear Polish poetry? I don't speak Polish. You are right, though; he was of Jewish descent. One of his ancestors was a Frankist who converted to Christianity."

"Who were the Frankists?" Zissel asked.

"Let's walk. I'll tell you about them on the way. I can't stand still any longer."

As they walked from street to street, Shlomo told Zissel about Shabtai Tzvi and Yaakov Frank, the false messiahs who eventually converted—the former to Islam and the latter to Christianity—after sewing the seeds of destruction in a multitude of Jewish communities.

"Jews either believed in them adamantly or violently opposed them," explained Shlomo. "The Jews of the Diaspora were drowning in a sea of never-ending troubles, and they clutched at any straw that might save them. They were easily taken in by these false messiahs. Today those episodes are all but forgotten, but at the time they threatened to destroy many Jewish communities. Husbands and wives, fathers and sons found themselves split over the controversy. Countless families were ruined."

Zissel, who had never studied any Jewish history, was all ears. Shlomo spoke only Yiddish, but she was able to speak with him thanks to her grandparents who had spoken to her in Yiddish as long as they were alive. Now she was especially grateful for this heritage. If not for them, she would not have been able to communicate with Shlomo at all.

As long as he was involved in his story, Shlomo had paid no attention to his surroundings. When he was finished, he suddenly noticed where they were and an expression of awe and surprise crossed his face. Zissel asked why.

"This is exactly the place I wanted to see. As Hillel said, 'My feet bring me to the place that I love,' " said Shlomo, quoting Tractate *Sukkah*.

"What's so special about this building?" asked Zissel.

"This is the synagogue of the Rama," he answered.

"Is there any lack of synagogues in Cracow? We must have passed at least half a dozen as we walked."

"This is not just any synagogue. This one is special."

"Why?" she asked.

Shlomo began to tell Zissel about the Rama, "The day-to-day life of every Polish Jew and of many other Jews as well, is dictated by the works of Rabbi Moshe Isserles of Cracow. He condensed the whole Torah into his books and lit the way for observant Jews all over Europe." Shlomo paused and added, "I want to go into the synagogue and put on *tefillin*."

"Why didn't you put on your *tefillin* in the morning?" asked Zissel. "It's almost noon. What happened to you?"

"I guess I forgot," mumbled Shlomo.

"What? How could you forget something you've been doing for so many years?"

"Well, when I used to sit in the *Beith Midrash* in Chedalonova, more than once it happened that I became so absorbed in the *gemara* that I forgot to eat. I suppose one can forget spiritual needs as well as he can physical ones."

Zissel laughed. "You have an answer for everything."

In his heart Shlomo knew that she was right. The true reason for his forgetfulness was that Shlomo of the Moadon had not wanted to put on *tefillin*. But facing the Rama Synagogue, Shlomo of the *Beith Midrash* once again had the upper hand.

"Wait here for me," he said to Zissel, "while I go into the synagogue for a few minutes."

Shlomo entered the synagogue, inspired by the holiness of the site. He turned to the caretaker and asked if he could borrow a pair of *tefillin*. The *shammash* eyed him suspiciously, but finally gave him the *tefillin*. Shlomo put them on and recited the *Shema* and *Shemoneh Esrey* prayers. Then he left.

"Let's go back to the hostel," he said. "We have to continue our journey this afternoon."

Zissel studied Shlomo's face and saw that some change had taken place in him. In the morning he had been restless and distracted. Even while he was telling her about the false messiahs, he had been preoccupied. He was in one place while his thoughts were in another. Something had been bothering him. Now he was different. His peace of mind was mirrored in the expression on his face.

Shlomo and Zissel returned to the hostel, and after dinner and a short rest, the *chalutzim* continued their trip.

✱ 7 ✱ *The End of the Trip*

On the train, the *chalutzim* had time to become better acquainted. In Cracow they had split up into small groups to go sight-seeing, spending only mealtimes together. Now, as some sixty-odd *chalutzim* were crowded together into three railway coaches, they began to form friendships.

In Trieste, they joined the hundreds of others already housed in the Jewish Agency transit camp, all awaiting their turn to set sail for Eretz Yisrael. A ship left every two weeks. Some *chalutzim* were lucky and received a place on board after only a few days' wait; others had to wait weeks. This was a typical youth camp. Each morning began with exercises. Between breakfast and lunch, the *chalutzim* either participated in various sports or went sight-seeing in town. Those who were tired of both activities would spend the morning at the port, watching the ships and marveling at the sea. For most of them, this was their first encounter with the sea. Some had not even lived in the vicinity of a small river. Thus the sea was a novel experience, and they did not want to be afraid of it when they began the long boat voyage to Eretz Yisrael.

Between lunch and supper, the program was the same as

it had been in the morning. The food, too, was the same, just as it had been in Cracow. Occasionally, a bit of meat was served at lunch. When they had nothing left to do but await their turn to set sail, the *chalutzim* would sit around the camp and engage in interminable discussions on one subject only—ideology. These ideological discussions invariably turned into debates, as there were almost as many ideological positions as there were *chalutzim*. Shlomo had thought that they were all united under one flag. Now he learned that for some *chalutzim* the blue in their flag was a strong, deep blue like the sky in Eretz Yisrael. For others it was a pale blue like the sky in the diaspora. Shlomo found out that there were even some *chalutzim* who did not accept Hebrew as their national tongue. They thought that Yiddish should be the Jewish national language. This he could not understand. He learned that these *chalutzim*, the Poalei Zion, had initially been opposed to Zion. After a while Shlomo gave up trying to figure out such an impossible puzzle.

For some of the *chalutzim* the return to Zion was their main goal; for others it was subordinate to the cause of social justice. For still others it was not even of secondary importance, as they were totally devoted to the ideal of equality among mankind.

When Shlomo asked one of them why in the world he wanted to go to Palestine when he could find all the equality one could desire in the Soviet Union, he was told, "You are right. But instead of my going to Soviet Russia, I intend to bring Soviet Russia to Eretz Yisrael. The revolution of the masses must encompass the whole world."

Shlomo could not accept such an answer. One did not

have to go all the way to Eretz Yisrael to promote the Soviet Revolution. This could be done in Poland, too. Shlomo thought to himself, "The blue in his flag is so washed out that it looks more like the white of surrender than the blue and white flag of rebirth."

Since Zissel had found many Polish-speaking friends in the camp she no longer spent so much time with Shlomo. It was much easier for her to express herself in Polish than in Yiddish, especially now that Shlomo had even begun trying to speak in Hebrew. When the *chalutzim* first heard Shlomo's Hebrew they burst out laughing at his Ashkenazic accent. Embarrassed, Shlomo retorted, "Were it not for the Holy Tongue heard in the *Beith Midrash* and synagogue, there would *be* no Hebrew language for you to speak!"

Lately, Shlomo had begun to walk around bareheaded. Nevertheless, when he heard any of the *chalutzim* mocking the *yeshivah* world he would fiercely come to its defense. He spent many hours in introspection, torn between two extremes. Sometimes he had an overwhelming desire to go back to the *yeshivah*, and other times he felt compelled to flee as far as possible from it. Distressed and worn out by the terrible struggle within himself and realizing that he could not just return to his old place in the *Beith Midrash* as if nothing had happened, he decided that he must cut off all his ties with his past. He must remove himself completely from anything that might remind him of the *Beith Midrash*. In one corner of his suitcase were a pair of *tzitzith* and the precious set of *tefillin* his father had bought him for his *bar mitzvah*. When he left Chedalonova it would never have occurred to him that he could do without them, but now he began to consider the possibility. When he tried to take them out of his suitcase, however, his hand refused to obey him. He could not bear to touch the *tefillin.* With a sigh, Shlomo said to himself, "I am destined to struggle with myself. My suffering is not yet over."

One day, the names were announced of those who were to set sail for Eretz Yisrael on the morrow. Zissel heard her name called. Afraid that she would have to travel alone, she listened nervously to the rest of the list until finally, Shlomo's name was also called, and she let out a sigh of relief. That day was a holiday for all those would be on the boat. After packing their meager belongings and eating supper, they gathered together in the camp yard and sang and danced late into the night.

In the morning all the *chalutzim* accompanied them to the boat. The new passengers boarded the ship and immediately went to the rails to catch a last glimpse of their friends in the port. When the gangplank was removed, they started to sing *Hatikvah.* But some, such as the Poalei Zion, sang with no enthusiasm, barely opening their mouths. As the boat began to move away from the port, everyone waved.

Even when the boat was far away and they could no longer see their friends, the *chalutzim* remained on deck, staring at the sea and contemplating the future. Their homes, their family and friends, the country where they had been born and had grown up—all this was behind them. They were now beginning a new life. Would they ever come back here?

Finally, they went below deck to examine their new living quarters. There were several large cabins, each holding a few dozen passengers. There were also smaller first-class cabins for the tourists and merchants who were used to living in comfort wherever they went.

Some of the ship's passengers were elderly men and women. For years they had been planning to go to Eretz Yisrael, and now, with their last ounce of strength, they were realizing their dream. They were familiar with our sages' dictum "Whoever is buried in Eretz Yisrael is considered as if he were buried under the Temple Altar (*Kethuboth* 111)." What better resting-place could there be for their weary bones than under the Temple Altar, in the very ground from which Adam had been created. Rambam wrote, "Man was created from the selfsame place from which he receives atonement" (*Mishneh Torah*, Laws of the Temple, ch. II).

Rabbi Meshullam Charif of Pogromova was one of the elderly people on board, although he was not old enough to be sailing toward death. But he had despaired of Poland and was fleeing to Eretz Yisrael after several Jews from his town were murdered by the Poles. He intended to settle in the holy city of Jerusalem and establish a *yeshivah* in memory of the Jews of Pogromova. He would devote himself to teaching Torah until God in His Grace would gather in all the exiles and redeem His land and His people.

Rabbi Meshullam didn't wait to arrive in Jerusalem in order to begin teaching Torah. The first day on board he had gathered together all the old men and formed a *shiur*. His group also prayed together, morning and evening, in one corner of the deck. Since they were only nine men they had to recruit a tenth from among the non-observant passengers, but the *chalutzim* would not agree to join the *minyan*. They were opposed to prayer on principle, and always went bare-headed. It was no coincidence that Shlomo was never on deck at prayer time. He knew very well that they needed a tenth man for a *minyan.* Were they to approach him he would have to decide one way or the other. He knew that he would not be able to refuse, so he chose to stay below deck.

Once, Shlomo put on his cap and joined the *gemara* lesson. He had heard of Rabbi Meshullam Charif years ago in Chedalonova and was eager to hear him in person. The passage they were learning was familiar to Shlomo and he could not restrain himself from asking the *Rav* a question. The *Rav* paused, surprised, and exclaimed, "You have asked well, my son!"

Even before the *Rav* could word his answer, Shlomo countered with an answer of his own. Now the *Rav* was really amazed. Whether or not this was the answer that he himself had intended to give, he now added nothing. Instead he said, "I can see that you are a *talmid chacham.* Why don't you join our *minyan?*"

Shlomo hesitated, and then replied, "Our sages of blessed memory stated in *Pesachim,* 'One who has studied and then deserted the Torah is worse than all others.' "

Hearing such a cynical answer, the *Rav* looked closely at Shlomo. What he saw was suffering and sadness, not mockery.

"If you know the teachings of our Rabbis, then why don't you return to our Torah?" asked the *Rav.*

Shlomo answered slowly. "A man's soul is very complex. Some things are within man's control, yet they are not. Life is not simple."

"Explain yourself," urged the *Rav*.

But Shlomo would not. Instead, he left the group.

On the seventh day, those on deck saw the first houses of Haifa on the horizon. They ran to spread the news that the end of their trip was near. All rushed on deck to catch their first glimpse of Eretz Yisrael. The port seemed to be approaching them rapidly. Shlomo, very excited, stood beside the rail, absorbed in himself. His head was filled with so many different, contradictory thoughts that he was overwhelmed. He couldn't even tell which thoughts were his own and which were foreign to him. So absorbed in himself was he that he didn't even notice Zissel at his side until she asked, "What strange thoughts are you thinking, Shlomo?"

"What?" asked Shlomo, startled.

"Now that we've arrived at our destination, we should rejoice and prepare ourselves for practical deeds. Put your disturbing thoughts aside," said Zissel gently.

Shlomo sighed. "You are right, of course. The first thing we must do when we get off the ship is write to our parents. When we wrote last week from Trieste, we had no return address to send them. I am very anxious to hear how things are at home. These are troubled times for the Jews in Poland, and I am worried about the people of Chedalonova."

"Yes," said Zissel, "I will write home first thing. I miss my parents very much. We left home only a short time ago, but it seems like years have passed."

The ship cast anchor, the gangplank was lowered and passengers began to alight. The first of the *chalutzim* were already standing on the soil of Eretz Yisrael.

✷ 8 ✷ *The Death of Edmond Blitz*

The situation in Poland was bad. Since Hitler's ascent to power in Germany, conditions in Poland had worsened from day to day. Anti-Semitism had ancient roots in Poland and appeared in many guises. In times of trouble, when the Polish eagle was preyed upon by her ever-hungry neighbors and Poland was in danger of being torn to bits, the Poles would bury their hatred for the Jews and share their troubles as if they were brothers. At such times the Polish national poets even spoke of the redemption of Poland and of Israel in one breath. But the hatred remained hidden deep in their hearts, silent, waiting. When the day came that Poland gained the upper hand and was free again, the old hatred for the Jews would ooze out of the hidden places in Polish hearts until it overflowed. Now, ever since Hitler had legitimized the spilling of Jewish blood, Poland was eager to follow the German example. True, the Poles had always hated the Germans, who were constantly trying to cut Poland into pieces. They had successfully done so three times in the last two hundred years. Now again, for a fourth time, the Germans were threatening Polish sovereignty. Nevertheless, as far as the "Jewish problem" was concerned, the Poles were in complete agreement with the Germans. They were quite willing to drive the Jews out of Poland, just as the Germans were doing in Germany.

The trouble was that the situation in the two countries was not the same. The Germans could claim that many of the Jews were not true German citizens and therefore had no right to remain in Germany. Either they themselves, or their fathers or grandfathers before them, were foreigners who had emigrated from Poland and settled illegally in Germany. Therefore they could be sent back where they came from. The Jews of Poland, however, had lived in the country for over a thousand years.

Nevertheless, the Poles did not give up. If they couldn't actually expel the Jews, they could at least make them feel highly unwelcome. For instance, two strong young Poles would stand outside every Jewish store, bearing a large placard. It was illegal discrimination to prohibit customers from shopping in Jewish stores—and it would also paint a poor public image of Poland internationally—but there was no law against putting up a sign stating that a certain store was owned by a Jew. The point was obvious. If, despite the placard, some good-hearted Pole would attempt to patronize the store, the sign holders would take a few steps forward and block the entrance, managing not to notice that someone was trying to get inside. No one could be arrested for misunderstanding another person's intentions. Hearts do not stand trial.

Thus, the Jewish stores stood empty all day long. Merchandise lay untouched on the shelves, as worthless as an unturned stone. When the shop owners' bills were due, they found themselves penniless. One might ask why they didn't make a living from one another. After all, *Jews* could not be prevented from entering Jewish stores. Three thousand years ago, when the sages had come to King David with a similar problem, he had advised them to make a living from one another. Even then they had objected to this piece of advice, stating: "A handful cannot satisfy a lion" (*Berachoth* 3).

The situation degenerated so, that some Jews began to think of emigrating to a friendlier country. The vast majority, however, were unable to do so. They remained in their own places and accepted their misfortune.

The hatred of the Poles, when they saw that they had not succeeded in driving the Jews out of Poland, knew no bounds. What *chutzpah* these Jews had—opening their stores in the morning and closing them in the evening as if everything were 'business as usual'. It was as if keeping their stores open was more important to them than the business itself. This was an open provocation, as if the Jews were proclaiming to the Poles: You want us to run away, but we will not budge, for Poland belongs to us!

Could there be any greater *chutzpah* than that of a Jew who claims that Poland belongs to *him* and not to the Poles? A money-hungry Jew—a Shylock—might possibly be forgiven, but not a Jew so stubborn as to keep his store open in the face of Polish objection.

The Poles' anger grew to murderous proportions. They set aside their placards and took up clubs instead. Some of these clubs were used on the heads of the Jews of Chedalonova.

One incident involved Zissel's father, the lawyer Edmond

Blitz. Two members of the Jewish Bund approached two Poles who were blocking the entrance to Moscovitz's store. "You are breaking the law," said the Bundists. "It is prohibited to boycott a store."

"We are not boycotting the store," retorted the Poles. "We are simply proclaiming that this store is owned by a Jew."

"It is forbidden to boycott indirectly," said the Bundists.

"Who are you to teach us what Polish law forbids?"

"We are citizens of Poland," answered the Jews, "just like you. And we wish to cure the social ills of our country."

At that, the Poles' blood began to boil. They were speechless. But actions speak louder than words, and without wasting words, they took justice into their own hands. The two poor Bundists were badly beaten and only managed to escape thanks to a few Jewish bystanders who came to their aid.

The Bundists spent several days in bed. When they were back on their feet, they approached Edmond Blitz and retained him as their lawyer in a suit against the Poles who had beaten them.

The trial took place a few days later in a courtroom packed with Poles, a few Jews interspersed among them. Edmond Blitz represented Aryeh and Ze'ev, the Bundists. The lawyer Polinski represented Stashek and Yantek. One of the Bundists was called to the witness stand to tell his story. Then the lawyer began to cross-examine him.

"Your words were an open provocation, purposely intended to incite these two upright Polish citizens to violence. You were just asking for a fight," accused Polinski.

"What kind of provocation are you talking about?" asked Ze'ev.

"That statement of yours 'We are Polish citizens just like you are,'" answered Polinski.

"Yes," said Ze'ev, "that's what I said. But that's no provocation. That's the truth."

"No," said Polinski. "That is not the truth. Poland belongs to the Poles—not to the Jews. Even if you are legally Polish citizens, you are still merely guests in Poland. The comparison that you drew was insulting, and one which the Polish people cannot forgive."

"I am no guest in Poland. I was born here and have never lived anywhere else," protested Ze'ev.

"You only happened to be born in Poland because your father happened by chance to be in Poland at the time of your birth. And your father only happened to be born in Poland because his father chanced to be staying in Poland when *he* was born. Even if your family happened to have lived in Poland for a thousand years, you would nevertheless remain guests, not true Poles."

Edmond Blitz tried to correct Polinski. "Assimilation is a perfectly natural phenomenon. People whose fathers and grandfathers were born in Poland—people who speak Polish, are educated in Polish schools, and are at home in the Polish culture—are Poles in every respect. No discrimination should be made between them and between Poles of Slavic origin."

At these words a murmur ran through the crowd. Edmond Blitz's comments had made their ears ring. That Ze'ev the Bundist could speak of equal rights and Polish citizenship for both Poles and Jews—that might be understandable. But to speak of Poles of Jewish origin and Poles of Slavic origin—as though the Polish nation was a conglomerate of two races—that was absolutely too much. The audacity of this "*Jid*" who considered himself Polish infuriated them.

Then it was Stashek's turn at the witness stand. He told the following story.

"Yantek and I stood peacefully beside the store of the *Jid* Moscovitz. We held a placard stating that this was a Jewish store, so that people could decide for themselves whether they wanted to shop there or not. Along came these two Jews" (here he pointed at Ze'ev and Aryeh) "and provoked us until they made our blood boil! What happened afterwards we can't even remember."

The cross-examination began. Polinski asked, "How exactly did the Jews provoke you?"

Stashek answered, "They told us that they had come to correct the social injustices in Poland."

"Come where?" asked Polinski.

Stashek hesitated and then answered, "They said they had come to Poland to cure the social injustice here."

Here Edmond Blitz objected, "Did they say that they had come to Poland—or to the boycotted store—to cure the social injustice there?"

"They were obviously saying they had come to Poland to correct the social injustice here," replied Stashek.

This answer aroused the audience to a state of agitation. The Poles were furious at the Jews' insulting comment that they had come to Poland to cure its social injustices. The verdict was to be pronounced in two days' time. Nevertheless, it was already perfectly clear what the verdict would be. Whenever Polinski took the stand, the judge would look directly at him, nodding his head in agreement as he listened. Whenever Edmond Blitz spoke, the judge turned his cold eyes on the empty space in the middle of the hall, his face a wax mask.

Two days later, the townspeople of Chedalonova assembled in the Court Hall to hear the verdict. No Jews were present. They had already read the verdict in the judge's eyes during the cross-examination. While waiting for the judge, the Poles in the courtroom repeated Stashek's testimony, egging each other on with comments about the insolence of the "*Jids.*" Polinski and Blitz sat, each one in his own seat, as if the other did not exist. Ze'ev and Aryeh sat in their chairs, their eyes betraying their fear of the future. Stashek and Yantek sat looking as though they were at a wedding, their faces beaming with joy.

When the judge entered the courtroom, a tension-filled silence spread through the room. He took out a document and began to read:

"The accused Stashek and Yantek are found innocent of the charges pressed against them on the following grounds: Stashek's testimony rings true. It is not honorable for a Pole to lose control of himself to such an extent that he cannot even recall what he did. Yet even if we do accept the testimony of the prosecution that Stashek and Yantek actually did perform the acts of which they are accused, they cannot be blamed. It is well known that the Polish people defend their country's honor with all their might. Anyone who insults Poland must know that he will elicit a very strong reaction from the Poles—a reaction so strong that a Pole might not even recall what he did. The prosecution must apologize to the Polish people for their arrogance in claiming that they came to Poland to correct its social injustices. Poland has no need of strangers to help correct its social ills."

When the judge finished, a furor arose among the crowd in the courtroom. A hearty round of applause for his speech was mixed with cries of "*Jids* to Palestine!"

Who knows what might have befallen Edmond Blitz and the Bundists Ze'ev and Aryeh had not two policemen escorted them out of the courtroom and sent them home.

Edmond Blitz was heart-broken. That day, his entire world collapsed. For years he had tried to be a Pole in every possible way, and now the judge had ruled that he was only a stranger in Poland, not a real Pole at all.

For two days Edmond stayed away from his office. In no condition to work, he was completely disoriented and incapable of concentrating. Finally, on the third day, making a tremendous effort to pull himself together, he forced himself to go to work.

When he didn't return home on time, Rozeshka went to the office to find him. Upon entering his room, she found her husband slumped in his chair, his head leaning against the backrest, as if he were asleep. When she came up to him and gently tapped his shoulder to wake him up, he fell out of the chair. Hearing Rozeshka's screams, the neighbors came running in. Someone ran to call the Jewish doctor, Raphael Gutheartz. One look at Edmond was sufficient for the doctor to pronounce him dead. After examining the body thoroughly, he saw the small round hole in Edmond's skull. But no weapon could be found.

"Blitz did not die," the doctor announced. "He was murdered."

The entire Jewish community of Chedalonova attended the funeral. If during his lifetime Edmond Blitz had cut himself off from his people, he returned to them upon his death. A Jew who dies a martyr's death is forgiven all his sins and is called a *chassid*, a righteous person (*Sanhedrin* 47). And any Jew murdered by Gentiles simply because he was Jewish, has died a holy death. Jewish law states that he who dies *al kiddush haShem*, to sanctify God's name in this world, is a part of the Jewish community. Even those who had no contact with the deceased during his lifetime must now tear their clothing and mourn for him. And he must be eulogized in the synagogue and *Beith Midrash*.

The Jews of Chedalonova treated Edmond accordingly. At his funeral oration in the *Beith Midrash*, mention was made of the increasingly troubled times for the Jewish community. There were new signs every day. The Jews of Chedalonova were urged to strengthen their spirits and not, God forbid, fall into despair.

Rozeshka Blitz was left all alone. Zushka had left home for Eretz Yisrael, and she had no one to comfort her in her heartbreak. She had no friends among the Jewish women of Chedalonova, having purposely cut herself off from the Jewish community, just as her husband had done. All of her friends were Polish. But now the Polish women wouldn't even look at her. Since the trial she was no longer a Pole but a Jewess—no better than any of the others. She had no family in Chedalonova either. There was no way out. Zushka must come home. Rozeshka was sure her daughter would come when she heard what had happened. She must notify Zushka of the tragedy, but how could she, when she hadn't yet received any mail and didn't know her daughter's address?

Rozeshka went to visit Mrs. Sharfson to ask if she had received a letter from Shlomo, but her answer, too, was negative. She even went to the Moadon Hechalutz to ask how to address her letter, but they also told her that it was too early to write to Zushka in Eretz Yisrael. She might even still be on the boat. There was nothing to do but to wait patiently for Zushka's first letter with a return address. Rozeshka had no strength to wait patiently. She could do nothing but sit forlornly alone, yearning impatiently for the first letter from her beloved daughter.

✷ 9 ✷ *Kibbutz Dath Ha'avodah*

Not all of the *chalutzim* had the same destination. There were those who turned to the *kibbutzim* and *moshavim* to work the land, and there were others who went to the villages or to the city to do manual labor — each according to his training and experience. Shlomo and Zissel went to Kibbutz Dath Ha'avodah. Zissel worked in the children's house while Shlomo, who had not yet mastered any particular skill, worked at a different job every day.

The *kibbutz* was large, with room for a wide spectrum of opinions. Everyone agreed that work was their "religion," but some were more "religious" than others. Those who believed devoutly worked even on Shabbath, and with religious fervor. Those who were less devout also worked on Shabbath, but only because they could not distinguish between the holy and the profane.

There were other differences of opinion among the members of the *kibbutz*, such as their attitude toward the Arabs. The *chalutzim* whose only religion was work, could not forgive the Arabs for letting the country lie desolate for so many centuries. Even now, the work of the Arabs brought no blessing to the land. Content to continue in their traditional ways, the Arabs would never build up the country or make the wilderness flower. Therefore, these *chalutzim* did not value the Arabs, their work or their opinions. They considered Eretz Yisrael their own, and they felt free to build it as they wished.

On the other hand, there were *chalutzim* who believed fervently that equality was also a supreme value, and they were troubled by the knowledge that their lives were more comfortable than those of the Arab villagers. Furthermore, now that they were in Eretz Yisrael, they saw things differently than they had in Chedalonova, Nachrovah and Temyonovah. There, they could only imagine what Eretz Yisrael was like; here, they were confronted with reality, and there is a tremendous difference between imagination and reality. What can be built by one's imagination in an hour may take a thousand years to build in reality. In their imagination, life in Eretz Yisrael had appeared idyllic, but in reality nothing is ideal. Before arriving in Palestine, they had imagined that *chalutzim* worked all day long, singing and dancing in their free time. Now that they were actually living in Eretz Yisrael, they were confronted with the truth—not everyone was a worker. There were small businessmen and rich merchants. One could even eke out a living at unproductive labor such as selling cold drinks.

And there was unemployment. While some people were indeed singing and dancing, others were sighing because they had looked for work but couldn't find any. In short, there was no equality in life, a fact which disturbed the peace of mind of the *kibbutzniks*. The *kibbutzim* had equality, but how could they come to terms with the world outside the *kibbutz*?

Shlomo also could find no peace of mind. He was not disturbed by the conflict between the religions of work and equality, but by the conflict between the *kibbutz* and the *Beith Midrash*. He was still torn between two worlds and neither would relinquish its hold on him.

One day the news spread in the *kibbutz* that riots had broken out in several areas in Eretz Yisrael. Arabs had murdered a number of Jews, and the Jews had retaliated vigorously.

Tempers rose on the *kibbutz*. A small minority defended the Arabs, saying that they were not to blame for their violence. They felt that they were being driven off their land. They should not be held responsible if their discontent caused them to overreact and to take revenge.

But this was a small minority. The vast majority of the *kibbutz* members joined the Haganah to defend the Jewish homeland in Eretz Yisrael. Those who had defended the Arabs began to feel uncomfortable on the *kibbutz*; they were like outcasts. Their friends avoided them and considered them traitors to the Jewish cause. Gradually they realized that they would have to leave the community, but there was nowhere for them to go. They knew that there was no point in going to a different *kibbutz*, for the situation would be the same wherever they went. Neither did they wish to move to the city. After all, they were *chalutzim*, and their place was in the fields. But the more the riots spread, and the more Jewish blood was spilt,. the worse their position in the *kibbutz* became.

Finally, the minority group called a meeting to decide what to do. One of the group, Elka of Temyonovah, said,

"Apparently we were mistaken. The only place in the world that will ever be a true home for us is the Soviet Union. There, honesty and justice, equality and freedom, rule supreme. That is the only place for true lovers of peace. If we really want to live a good life we must leave Palestine and go to Russia."

Elka's words struck her listeners like thunder. They shocked, but in some hearts, they rang true. And eventually, they convinced. There did not seem to be any other alternative. It had obviously been a mistake for these *chalutzim* to come to Palestine. They should have immigrated to the U.S.S.R. and taken part in the Workers' Revolution. Then, after the revolution, they could have come to Eretz Yisrael. What kind of life could one live in Eretz Yisrael without the Socialist Revolution? No, they were not giving the Jewish homeland up, but first they must bring the Socialist Revolution to the Jews. Then they would establish a binational Jewish-Arab state. They would even have two national languages: Yiddish and Arabic.

After a prolonged discussion in which everyone repeated and rephrased the same views, they agreed to Elka's proposal. It could not, however, be carried out immediately. They must prepare themselves.

Zissel was not disturbed by the state of affairs in Eretz Yisrael. She had not come searching for equality; she had come because of Shlomo. If nothing disturbed Shlomo, then nothing disturbed her either. She had already written a second letter to her parents and was awaiting their reply. Despite her intense homesickness, Zissel had no intentions of returning to Chedalonova. A letter from her parents would suffice to make her feel better.

Every day after work the daily mail was distributed. Zissel would stand, all ears, listening to the names of those lucky people who had received mail. When the whole list had been read and her name had not been called, she would sigh with disappointment.

One day, Zissel's name was called and she was given an envelope. She caressed the letter, but did not open it in public. Everything was common property on the *kibbutz* except one's emotions. This was her own private affair and she didn't intend to share it with anyone. Zissel went back to her room, where she could open the envelope in privacy. Before beginning to read it, she noticed spots on the paper, as though drops of water had fallen on it.

As Zissel read, her heart fell. The letter raised many more questions than it answered. Her mother was begging her to come home as soon as possible. Something had happened that her mother didn't want to write about, but Zissel would find out when she came. Zissel had also expected to receive a few lines from her father, but there were none. Could it be that he had not yet forgiven her for leaving home? Her father was a Polish patriot and he had considered her act a betrayal of the Polish homeland. Zissel smiled to herself at the thought. Her father had absolutely no idea of what a national Jewish homeland meant. The agitation in the Jewish world over the idea of a Jewish state had not touched him. To him, there was no Jewish problem. He didn't believe that there was any reason for the Jewish nation to continue to exist. Instead, all the Jews of Poland should become Poles; all the Jews of France, Frenchmen; the Jews of England,

Englishmen; and so on all over the world.

Very well. Her father was angry at the moment. Eventually, he would come to terms with his daughter and her "betrayal." She needn't take it too seriously. He would probably write a few lines in the next letter.

But what could have happened in Chedalonova? Why hadn't her mother explained in her letter? Perhaps it was only a trick to get her to come home. Her mother knew that if she wrote the whole story, it probably wouldn't be important enough to make Zissel return, so she only hinted dramatically at some imaginary catastrophe in her letter. Poor Mother. She must miss Zissel terribly. Zissel missed her too, but she still couldn't see herself going back to Poland.

Zissel sat in her room, weighing the pros and cons of the matter, unable to reach a decision. Finally, she had an idea. If she had received a letter from home, Shlomo might also have received mail. If something had really happened in Chedalonova, his parents would have written, and he would be able to tell her. When her letter had come, she had rushed immediately to her room, not waiting for all the mail to be distributed. She wasn't sure that Shlomo had received mail, but it was logical to assume so. Both their parents probably answered their letters the same day they received them.

Zissel ran to find Shlomo.

"What news did you get from home?" she asked.

"I haven't even received one letter yet," Shlomo replied. "Why do you ask?"

Disappointed, Zissel pulled her letter from her pocket and handed it to Shlomo.

Shlomo opened the letter, read it once, and then reread

it. At the second reading he understood that something of real import must have happened in Zissel's family. He noticed the spots on the paper and recognized them for what they were—dried tears. Returning the letter to Zissel, he said, "Perhaps I will get a letter tomorrow or the next day and then we'll know what happened." Disappointedly, Zissel pocketed the letter. Who knew when Shlomo would get mail? It might take more than just a day or two.

When he was alone, Shlomo began to think. He must prepare Zissel for bad news. If necessary, he could conceal whatever news he received from home. His mother wrote in Yiddish, and his father in Yiddish interspersed with phrases from the Holy Tongue. Zissel was just beginning to speak Hebrew and could read neither Hebrew nor Yiddish. She would certainly not be able to decipher his father's fancy rabbinic handwriting.

Nevertheless, he decided that it would be best to tell Zissel the whole truth when he found out what had happened so that she would fulfill her mother's request. Otherwise Zissel would never agree to go home. He himself didn't yet know exactly what had transpired, but Shlomo was sharp, and he realized that it was no mere caprice that had prevented Edmond Blitz from adding a few lines. Obviously, he had not written because he could not. A person who is even half alive can write at least a line or two. Therefore, reasoned Shlomo, Edmond Blitz was either dead or close to it.

The truth was that Shlomo really didn't want Zissel to go home. He knew that she cared for him and he had grown to care for her as well. More than once he had thought of asking her to marry him. Nevertheless, he did not want to be the cause of her refusing her mother's request. He couldn't place his own personal wishes above her poor mother's welfare.

All that evening Shlomo discussed the dangers facing Polish Jewry with Zissel. Esau was giving free reign to his murderous hands and the voice of Jacob could not silence them. The lives of Polish Jews were cheap. Every day there was a new incident in one place or another.

It took another week until Shlomo received a letter from home with the news of the trial and Edmond Blitz's death. During that week Shlomo had also begun to worry. If Zissel had already received mail and he had not, perhaps something really terrible had happened in Chedalonova. Now that he knew the whole story, he was filled with sorrow over the tragedy that had befallen Zissel's family.

He made a great effort and managed to tell Zissel the news. For days, she was in tears. She cried over the death of her father, but she was also unhappy because now she would have to return to Poland and to part from Shlomo. Shlomo tried to comfort her.

He also promised Zissel, "We are not parting permanently—only for a while. Go back home to your mother and convince her to come back to Eretz Yisrael with you. When you come back you will find me waiting." Forcing a smile, he added, "I'm sure no other girl will carry me off in the meantime!"

Even Zissel smiled through her tears.

Zissel had little to do to prepare for her trip. Shlomo took care of her tickets. She had no idea where the money even came from. He was not one to discuss his actions when it came to matters of charity. A few days later several members of the *kibbutz* accompanied Zissel to the port. When she reached the gangplank just before boarding the ship, Zissel and Shlomo looked into each other's eyes for a long time. One pair of eyes said, "Promise!" The other answered, "I promise."

Zissel boarded the ship, and on the verge of tears, she waved to Shlomo from the deck. He waved back, for from that distance, it was no longer possible to look into each other's eyes.

✱ 10 ✱ *Shlomo at the Western Wall*

When the news spread throughout the *kibbutz* that Elka and her group had decided to emigrate to Soviet Russia, the *kibbutz* members reacted very strongly. Some were so furious over this betrayal that their anger knew no bounds. Others were quite happy to be rid of Elka and her followers. They wanted to see the country purified from those rebellious sons whose hearts belonged to foreign masters. If they did not rejoice in the rebuilding of Eretz Yisrael, let them go. Let only those who were absolutely faithful to the Jewish homeland remain.

When it became known, however, that Shlomo was part of the group, many eyebrows were raised. This young man who still had the *Beith Midrash* deep in his heart, what in the world could he find in Bolshevik Russia where it was forbidden to even mention the word *Beith Midrash*? Some refused to believe that Shlomo was really leaving, while others simply said, "Poor fellow! So much learning has confused him completely; he cannot tell his left hand from his right."

The members of the *kibbutz* had often asked Shlomo whether he had been to Jerusalem yet. When he would answer in the negative, they would look at him quizzically and ask, "Not even once?"

"Haven't you even gone to the Western Wall once?" asked Shmuel of Nachrovah. "How do you explain that? Every observant Jew the world over would give fortunes to see the Wall or touch its stones. They cannot, because they are so far away, but you—you who live in Eretz Yisrael—why haven't you ever gone to the Wall?"

The longer Shmuel went on with his teasing, the harder Shlomo tried to compose a convincing answer. Finally, he said, "The Wall doesn't have the same significance for you that it does for me. To you it is a historical site as interesting as any other site described in your history books. But to me, the Wall is not merely a historical site; it is a Holy Place. The Divine Presence has never left there. One must prepare himself before he approaches such a place. One cannot take his knapsack and walking stick and hike over to a place like the Temple Mount. The profane and the holy do not mix. But one day, when I am ready, I will go up to Jerusalem and kiss the stones of the Wall." As he spoke, Shlomo himself became convinced by his enthusiastic speech.

When he was all alone, Shlomo admitted to himself that this was not the real reason for his hesitation. In truth, he had not even begun to prepare himself to go up to Jerusalem. His real reason for postponing the visit was his fear that the stones of the Wall would not allow him to return to the *kibbütz*, and that he would not be strong enough to resist their pull. The Wall must be a much stronger spiritual force than the *Beith Midrash*. If he was still fighting to escape the influence of the *Beith Midrash*, how would he be able to resist the Wall?

But, after his inspiring speech to Shmuel, he had no

choice but to go up to Jerusalem at least once. There must be an end to his preparations.

One day, Shlomo made his trip. He left early in the morning so as to be back home by dark. One bus took him to the crossroads and another brought him to Jerusalem.

Once in the city, Shlomo did not go straight to the Wall. He postponed the confrontation as long as possible. First he headed for the Jewish Quarter of the Old City, walking through the crowded narrow alleyways and examining the houses, stores and workshops from the outside. What surprised him most was the large number of synagogues, *Batei Midrash* and *yeshivoth*. He would never have guessed that there could be so many synagogues and houses of learning in such a small area. Back in Chedalonova, he had heard of some of the more famous ones, such as the Churvah of Rabbi Yehuda *heChassid*. But here he found many synagogues and *yeshivoth* he had never heard of. Shlomo walked around, trying to see everything. Everywhere, he found people learning. Some were younger and some older, some were reciting *Tehillim* and others learning *mishnah*; some were learning *gemara* while others discussed the commentaries of Tosaphoth and Maharsha. It was such a warm, familiar atmosphere—an entire self-contained world, free of problems and doubts—not wrestling with itself, not struggling or searching for solutions to the riddle of Man and his world. This was a straight, paved road that one could safely follow.

Shlomo peered inside many buildings, but he didn't stop. Finally, he said, "I must go to the Wall. It's already late. By the time I get home it will be dark."

Passing one house with open windows, Shlomo heard a familiar voice. He paused for a minute to listen, trying to identify the speaker. Then, unable to resist, he entered the building, suddenly realizing it was a *Beith Midrash.* A few fifteen- and sixteen-year-old boys were sitting on benches around a medium sized table, their *gemaroth* open before them. At the head of the table sat Rabbi Meshullam Charif, explaining a passage to his students. They were so absorbed in their learning that they didn't even notice Shlomo, who took a seat on the end of one of the benches. The boy next to him gave him a passing glance and quickly turned back to his *gemara.*

Shlomo sat and listened. Rav Meshullam's voice was pleasant, and the eternal tune of the *gemara* sounded very sweet. Shlomo thought of the *Beith Midrash* in Chedalonova. He remembered his revered Rav with his long beard, surrounded by young boys, one of whom was Shlomo. He was filled with longing for those days, the best years of his life.

"Why did I ever leave? What have I found to replace that world?" he asked, unable to answer his own questions. The voices of the *Rav* of Chedalonova and Rav Meshullam merged as Shlomo was in both places at once. How good he felt. He had come home. Everything that had passed over him since he left the *Beith Midrash* in Chedalonova until now had been a nightmare. No, he had never really left, and therefore there was no need to return. Suddenly, the *Rav* was silent.

Just as Shlomo began to wonder why the tune had been interrupted, he felt a hand on his shoulder. He pulled himself out of his revery, focused his eyes, and saw Rav Meshullam before him. The *Rav* had looked up from his *gemara* to explain a difficult point and had seen Shlomo. Recognizing him immediately, he stopped the lesson, stood up and came over to him. For a few seconds, Shlomo was confused and disoriented; but he quickly pulled himself together, and stood up in deference to the Rav.

"How good that you have come to us," said the *Rav*. "You belong here. There are many young people who are beset by doubts and must struggle with themselves, but if they have learned Torah, the Torah comes to their aid and brings them back to themselves."

All the students were staring at Shlomo. He was not dressed like a *yeshivah* student. Where had the *Rav* made his acquaintance? What did he mean by "young people beset by doubts"? What kind of doubts? If the doubts revolved around Jewish law, why did he specify *young* people beset by doubts? Even *talmidei chachamim* and heads of *yeshivoth* had to wrestle with difficult questions. These youngsters were not aware of any other kind of doubts. They knew that there were religious and nonreligious Jews, but neither of these was in doubt. Each believed firmly in his own way.

Before returning to his seat at the head of the table, the *Rav* spoke to Shlomo again. "You will stay with us?"

"I am on my way to the *Kothel*," answered Shlomo. "That is why I came to Jerusalem."

"Then after you visit the Wall," said the Rav, "come back to us. We will find you a place among us. This is the younger group, but there are older students here for you to learn with. You need not worry about money. Our students receive free board and lodging."

Shlomo listened but did not answer. Then he said "*Shalom*" and left the *Beith Midrash*. Suddenly he realized how hungry he was. He had not eaten since early morning. He took out a few slices of bread and some olives he had brought with him from the *kibbutz* and found himself a place to sit on some stairs in an alleyway near the Dung Gate. When he finished eating, he got up to go to the Wall.

As he approached the *Kothel*, Shlomo saw a few old men standing on one side and a few old women on the other. "Why don't they put up a *mechitzah* between the men and women here, just as there is in a synagogue?" he wondered.

He noticed that some of the men were sitting on the ground. "They must be too old and tired to stand for long," he thought. "But why don't the Rabbis of Jerusalem set up a few benches for these old people who must be regular visitors here?"

Gazing at the Wall itself, Shlomo lifted his head up to count the rows of huge stones. Above and behind the top rows, he saw a shining golden dome. Moving back a bit to get a better view, he caught sight of a second, smaller dome of silver. Shlomo wanted to see these domed buildings. He went through one of the narrow passageways to the left of the Wall leading to the Temple Mount. At the entrance, an Arab asked him what he was looking for. Shlomo, who didn't understand Arabic, kept on walking. The Arab pushed him backwards hard, causing Shlomo to trip and fall.

Picking himself up, Shlomo returned to the Wall, and looked for an Ashkenazic Jew who spoke Yiddish and could explain what was happening. The Ashkenazim and the Sephardim dressed differently, so he had no trouble singling out two Ashkenazic Jews. But one was leaning against the Wall, lost in meditation, and the other was deep in prayer. Shlomo stood there, waiting. Finally the man who was praying took three steps backwards, bowed to his left, to his right, to the front and took three steps forward. He had completed the *Shemoneh Esrey*. Then he recited the concluding prayer, *Aleinu*.

When he finished, Shlomo came up and asked his questions. The old man looked at Shlomo closely and said, "I see from your questions that you are new to this country. This may even be your first visit to the Wall."

"That is true," answered Shlomo.

"You see, my son, we are in exile, even in Eretz Yisrael. The Wall is still in exile, too, for the Arabs have proclaimed the Wall a holy Moslem site, and the British mandatory government supports them. They believe it is quite generous of the Arabs to allow us to pray here for a few hours every day. However, we are not allowed to bring so much as a stool, not to speak of chairs or benches, or a partition or curtain to separate the men from the women.

"Up there on the Temple Mount are two Arab mosques. They stand on the site where our *Beith haMikdash* once stood, before its destruction. Jewish law forbids us to enter the Temple Mount, and the Arabs make sure that this law is kept, even by those Jews who do not observe other laws of the Torah." These last words were accompanied by a bitter smile.

Listening to the old man, Shlomo felt his spirit darken within him. This was not the Wall he had dreamed of. In Chedalonova, he had pictured the Wall as the prize possession of the Jewish people, who guarded it with all their might and did not allow any strangers to defile it.

"The Temple Mount is ours alone! This is where Avraham brought Yitzchak as a sacrifice. This is where Shlomo *haMelech* built the First Temple and Zerubavel ben Shealtiel the Second Temple. What could this old Jew mean when he says that the Wall belongs to the Arabs? How had it fallen into their hands? Why was a Jew forbidden to even sit on a chair in front of the Wall?"

No, this wall did not uplift his spirit. Who could have dreamed that there could be places in Eretz Yisrael itself, where Jews were forbidden to trespass? This was something he had not imagined in his wildest dreams and which he could not fathom.

Even in Poland, in that wicked land where gentiles were free to murder Jews, there was no place officially forbidden to Jews.

The mandatory edict forbidding Jews to bring chairs to the Wall or to enter the Temple Mount sent Shlomo into a deep depression. He had fled Poland and come to Eretz Yisrael to become a free man—one who could not be brutalized by the strong hand of the Gentiles. Now, suddenly, he had discovered that the strong hand of the Gentiles reached even to Eretz Yisrael.

Shlomo had intended to recite a prayer beside the Wall. True, he was no longer in the habit of praying, but he thought that here he would feel differently. But now his desire to pray disappeared. His spirit rebelled, pulling him away from this place. The decision was growing within him to flee from all the Gentiles who were denying him his freedom. Where could he go? He would go to those who had completely thrown off *all* religion, and who did not discriminate between Jew and non-Jew; to a place where he would be able to live in a truly free society with no barriers between one man and the next. He would join Elka's group. In Soviet Russia he would at last find peace of mind.

There was, however, one thing that bothered him. He had promised Zissel he would wait for her. After a prolonged debate with himself, he decided that he had not made any *explicit* promise. True, his eyes had promised, but he had learned in the *gemara* that one's unspoken thoughts are not legally binding.

Shlomo himself was not really satisfied with this reasoning, until one day he received a letter from Zissel, a letter full of despair. Her mother wouldn't even consider coming to Palestine. She was totally committed to Poland and would not leave her homeland. "Although there are wicked Poles, there are also good Poles," her mother had said. "Everywhere in the world there are both good and bad people."

Zissel's letter cried despair from every line. All hope of returning was gone. There was nothing she could do.

When Shlomo finished reading, he thought, "Now that Zissel is not coming back, I won't be betraying her. She is the one who has left me; it is not I who am forsaking her." He felt very sorry for Zissel, but he was also relieved that his own dilemma had been resolved.

A few days later Elka's group left Palestine for the U.S.S.R. Shlomo went with them.

✶ II ✶ *The Ghetto*

Following the pact between Hitler and Stalin, Poland was split between Russia and Germany, and Chedalonova fell under Hitler's jurisdiction. The Jews of Chedalonova suffered the same fate as those of all the other towns under Nazi dominion. Their lives were worth less each day. Finally the bitter day came when they were confined in a ghetto. Two streets were allotted to house the entire Jewish population of Chedalonova and were closed off with barbed wire. All Jews were ordered to move into the ghetto within twenty-four hours. Any Jew who had not moved by Sunday, the Christian Sabbath, would be punished "with all due severity." The Nazis knew that this was sufficient. The Jews were terrified enough of "light" punishment by the Nazis. Threat of "serious" punishment would certainly send them scurrying into the ghetto.

Nevertheless, the Germans did not take anything for granted. They knew that Jews simply could not be trusted. Some might try to postpone their move for a day or two in defiance of the law. Therefore the Germans marched from one Jewish house to the next, "helping" the Jews leave their homes and move into the ghetto on Sunday, as required by law. The Germans knew that Jews had sharp minds and might find all sorts of excuses to exclude themselves from this edict, and they also knew that they, speaking only German, would not be able to understand the Jews' claims; therefore they took a few Poles with them to serve as interpreters.

When the Nazis entered the Jewish homes, they found them deserted. Some of the houses had even been emptied of their furniture. Most people, however, realizing how overcrowded the ghetto would be, had left their furnishings behind, hoping to reclaim them upon their return. The apartments all had one thing in common: they were in a state of utter chaos. Closets and drawers were left open, clothes were strewn all over. There had been no time to arrange things. Or perhaps, now that their whole world had been turned upside down, the Jews had lacked the presence of mind to leave things in order. In either case, chaos reigned.

The German and the Pole assigned to the apartment of Rozeshka Blitz found the door unlocked. Inside, Rozeshka and Zissel were sitting opposite each other at the table, Rozeshka mending socks and Zissel reading a book. The German could not believe his eyes. The nerve of these two Jewesses was unbelievable. They had not even bothered to hide; they had simply ignored the edict as though it did not exist. The German transferred his gun from his shoulder to his hand, and waited for the Pole to investigate.

"Didn't you hear of the edict commanding all Jews to move to the ghetto?"

"Yes," answered Rozeshka, "we heard."

"Then why didn't you move? You don't look as if you have the slightest intention of moving."

"That's right; we have no intention of moving to the Jewish ghetto."

"Do you want to be punished?"

"No, we do not deserve any punishment. The edict does not apply to us."

"Why not?"

"I am a Polish woman."

At that, the Pole, who knew Rozeshka, grinned and said, "The Polish court has already ruled that you are not Polish. Your husband has already been punished for his presumptions, and now you, pigheaded Jewess, will be punished for yours!"

The German stood on the side waiting for the conversation to terminate. Finally he asked what was going on. Hearing the Pole's explanation in his broken German, the Nazi picked up his gun and focused it on Rozeshka. At that, Zissel jumped up from her chair, grabbed her mother by the arm and dragged her out of the house.

That morning, before the Nazis' visit to their house, Zissel and Rozeshka had thoroughly discussed the entire subject, and now, once again, on their hurried way to the ghetto, Zissel took her mother to task for not wanting to be what she was—a Jew; and for trying to be something which she wasn't—a Pole.

Rozeshka and Zissel arrived in the ghetto empty-handed. Zissel suggested to her mother that they look for Shlomo's family, the Sharfsons, and ask to stay with them. Upon Zissel's return to Chedalonova from Eretz Yisrael, she had visited the Sharfsons and given them Shlomo's regards. From that time on, Zissel had become friendly with them.

They knew nothing of Shlomo's promise to Zissel, or that Zissel had followed Shlomo to Eretz Yisrael, but the mere fact that Shlomo and Zissel had been together in Eretz Yisrael was enough to endear her to them.

Zissel made a special effort to become close to Shlomo's family. She considered them her own relatives. And now, the ghetto edict had instilled new hope in her. Since the Germans had forced her mother to "become" a Jewess, perhaps she would finally agree to immigrate to Eretz Yisrael when they got out of the ghetto.

Bathsheva received Zissel and her mother warmly. Zissel, who had not yet lost hope of returning to Shlomo, considered this a good sign. It was as if she were already almost a part of his family.

Life in the ghetto grew worse from day to day. People were starving. The crowded conditions and filth had led to epidemics, and everywhere people were sick and dying. Little by little, despair took hold. Rozeshka, however, was not about to give up. After all, she came from a stubborn nation. Although she was being forced to live in the ghetto together with all the other Jews, it was her dream to leave before the other Jews did. Even if the other Jews stayed, *she* would leave. She could depend on her Polish friends. They would get her out. Not all the Polish women had alienated themselves from her after the trial. There were still some who considered her one of their own. Nevertheless, each additional day spent in the ghetto eroded her confidence.

One day, the door opened and Mrs. Chasidov, a Polish friend who had been faithful even after the trial, stood in the doorway. Surprised and delighted, Rozeshka jumped up and ran to the door. The two friends hugged and kissed each other, tears flowing from their eyes.

"I knew you would come!" cried Rozeshka.

Zissel also stood up, approached Mrs. Chasidov and shook her hand. The Polish woman looked around the room and sighed. Then she turned back to Rozeshka and said, "At least you have a room of your own."

"You are mistaken," said Rozeshka. "We are not alone in this room. A family with two children lives here, too. Just now they are out."

Remembering that she had forgotten to ask Chasidova to sit down, Rozeshka apologized, took her hand, led her to the table and offered her a chair.

"I can only stay a few minutes," said Chasidova.

"Every minute that you spend with me lightens my suffering," answered Rozeshka. "I have no friends here. Physically, I am in the ghetto, but my heart is outside. I belong with those outside."

"I must leave as quickly as possible, for my own good and also for yours," continued Chasidova.

"But, why?" asked Rozeshka.

"Listen, and I will tell you how I got into the ghetto and what I have heard."

Chasidova told the following story: When she came to the ghetto gate she found a Polish guard on duty—one of the German collaborators. She told him she wanted to enter the ghetto.

"I know that those on the inside want to get out," he said, "but I wasn't aware that there was anyone outside who wanted to get in! Whom do you want to visit? There are no

Poles here—only the damn Jews. What business do you have with them?"

"There is a Jewess here who owes me money," she had answered, "and I want to collect my debt."

"You want to collect a debt from a Jew?" he asked. "The Jews don't repay debts. If you wish, I'll call one of the Germans and he will collect your debt for you."

"No, no," said Chasidova, "if you call one of the Germans, I'll never get my money back. He may succeed in getting the money from the Jewess, but the money will go to his wife—not to me. The Germans are not too fond of Poles either."

"I promise you the German will give you your money," said the guard.

"No," said Chasidova. "Let me first try to collect the money without the Germans. If I don't succeed, I can always ask for their help."

The guard hesitated, scratched his head, and wondered if he could let this woman enter the ghetto. Finally, he replied, "All right. Go on in and try your luck. You should know, though, that in two hours there will be a rounding up of ghetto children. If the Germans catch you in the ghetto, both you and I will be in a lot of trouble."

Chasidova promised not to stay for long. She walked inside and began to look for Mrs. Blitz's apartment. She asked a few people in the street, but no one knew her. Meanwhile, time was running out. She had promised to leave shortly, and so only a few minutes remained for her to visit.

When Chasidova had finished her story, Rozeshka said,

"That is very discouraging. I am not afraid of the Nazis, but I cannot remain in the ghetto. There is not even anyone here for me to talk to. They all speak Yiddish. I am all alone here."

Chasidova answered, "In my opinion, you need not set yourself apart from the Jews. I would have come to visit you even if you considered yourself Jewish instead of Polish. I am full of pity for the Jews, suffering so much from the Germans. And the Germans are also the enemies of Poland."

Rozeshka, embarrassed by Chasidova's rebuke, lowered her eyes. For a minute, no one spoke. Then Chasidova added, "If you find a way to get out of here, I am willing to hide you in my house. After all, the Germans will only occupy Poland until the war is over, and that cannot go on forever. Maybe I can even help you escape."

With those words, Chasidova rose and offered her hand to Rozeshka. Rozeshka shook her hand again and again, without a word. She was too upset and depressed to speak. Finally, she succeeded in saying "Thank you." Rozeshka was very upset. The happiness she had felt just a few moments ago had faded away. Who knew if it would ever return.

Chasidova offered her hand to Zushka and said, "I will make you the same offer I made your mother. I will try to find a hiding place for both of you."

"Thank you," answered Zissel. "If there are still Poles like you, Poland is not yet lost. But I have no intentions of leaving the ghetto. My place is here among my fellow Jews."

The Polish woman looked at Zushka benignly and said, "May you be blessed, my daughter. If there are still Jews like you, hope is not yet lost for the Jewish people. No man should alienate himself from his people or his religion—no matter what. No one should—or can—run away from himself."

Rozeshka stood on the side listening, her heart weeping within her. She cried because her own daughter, her own flesh and blood, had betrayed her by identifying with the Jewish people, and she cried because even her loyal Polish friend considered her a Jewess and not a Pole. Never before had Rozeshka felt so alone.

After Chasidova left, Zissel ran to look for Bathsheva to warn her that there would be a search in the ghetto in less than an hour. The children of the ghetto were in danger, and a hiding place must be found for little Sarah. Zissel had not left earlier so that she could hear everything Mrs. Chasidov had to say to her mother. She was afraid her mother might not repeat the conversation exactly as it had taken place. Neither mother nor daughter had much faith in each other when it came to matters of Jewish identity. All that time, however, Zissel had been watching the door, hoping that Mrs. Sharfson would come in. Now she lost no time, and ran to look for the Sharfsons, who were visiting some neighbors in the house.

Zissel called Bathsheva out of the room and, in a trembling voice, told her the bad news. Bathsheva turned white. She immediately called her husband and told him what Zissel had said. Kolonymos was badly shaken. "The first thing we must do," he said, "is to spread the news throughout the ghetto."

Without losing a minute, he returned to the room he had just left and whispered the news, telling his neighbors to pass it on to all the inhabitants of the ghetto. When he came out of the room again, Bathsheva grabbed his arm and asked, "What shall we do?"

Kolonymos looked at his wife and answered, "What *can* we do?"

"We must find a hiding place for Sarah. Time is not standing still," cried his wife.

But Kolonymos stood still, helpless as the captain of a sinking ship at sea. "Where in the ghetto can there be a hiding place? Every hole is occupied by someone. There are no secret places."

"Maybe in the *Rav*'s house," suggested Zissel.

She wanted to say more, but Kolonymos was already gone. He ran into the room, grabbed Sarah's hand and ran with her to the *Rav*'s house. He had realized immediately that Zissel's suggestion held the key to Sarah's salvation.

The Jews of Chedalonova held their *Rav* in great esteem, and even in these troubled times had given him and his wife their own private room. The *Rav*'s children had grown up and moved away from Chedalonova, so that only he and his wife were left. Their room was very small, but it was enough for the two of them. In this same room, the *Rav* also taught Torah to his students. There were two beds, a table, one chair, and a small bench. It was so small that there was almost no room between the table near the door and the beds along the wall. Sarah could hide under the bed farthest from the door. Anyone entering the room and finding two old people there would probably not think of searching for children.

When Kolonymos hurriedly brought Sarah into the

Rav's room and told him the story, the *Rav* answered, "I will certainly do all I can to help save a Jewish soul." Then he sighed at the thought that he could not save more than one.

Little Sarah listened to the story her father told the *Rav*. She didn't understand everything, but what she did understand was enough to plant a deep fear in her heart, a fear reflected in her bright eyes. As soon as her father withdrew his hand from hers and told her that she must remain in the *Rav*'s house for a while, her tiny body began to quake. The *Rav* placed his hand on Sarah's small head and said, "Sarah'leh, God is with you. Don't be afraid. The *Rebbetzin* and I will take good care of you."

Sarah looked into the *Rav*'s generous eyes and saw his good-hearted smile and was calmed. Kolonymos said, "Sarah'leh, be a good girl and listen to everything the *Rav* and *Rebbetzin* tell you to do." Sarah nodded her head in assent and lowered her eyes.

When Kolonymos left, the *Rav* sat Sarah down on the bench beside him and said to her, "Soon it will be Purim. Come Sarah, tell us the story of Queen Esther. I'm sure you know it."

"Yes, I do," she answered, and proceeded to tell them all about Mordechai and Esther. When she had finished, the *Rav* said, "All those who hate the Jews will be punished, just as the wicked Haman was." He lifted Sarah's small head and looked into her eyes, his smile instilling confidence in her.

Then the *Rav* stood up, walked over to the window, and listened to the sounds from outside, sounds of alarm. People were not walking; they were running. Usually, people shut themselves up inside at night and did not walk outside in the ghetto streets. Tonight there was an unusual amount of movement.

"The news Kolonymos brought must be true, " thought the *Rav*. Taking Sarah's hand, he said, "Come, Sarah'leh, and I'll show you where you must hide for a little while. The *Rebbetzin* and I will sit here beside you and watch over you."

Sarah got up from the bench, walked over to the bed the Rav had indicated, and crawled underneath.

In a few minutes the ghetto was surrounded by Nazis and the hunt was on. Heartbroken cries of mothers whose children had been snatched away were mixed with the raucous cries of the Germans. Many children of the ghetto were taken away that night. Only a few were saved; Sarah was one of those few. As soon as the cries began, the *Rav* and the *Rebbetzin* sat down at the table facing each other like two old people with nothing to do. When the Nazis opened their door, they could only check the room from the doorway as the entrance was blocked by the table. Seeing a sleepy old couple, they slammed the door and left.

As soon as the hunt was over, Kolonymos ran back to the *Rav*'s house to see if all was well with Sarah. Catching sight of her father, little Sarah burst into tears. The *Rav* put his hand on her head and said, "Now, my daughter, you may cry."

At home, Bathsheva and Zissel waited impatiently. When Kolonymos arrived, he let Sarah walk into the room first. Bathsheva ran over to her, Zissel close behind, and little Sarah was overwhelmed with kisses from her mother, from Zissel, and even from Rozeshka. Sarah told them the story, happy that everyone was so pleased with her. After

Bathsheva had her fill of looking at the daughter who had miraculously been saved, she turned to Zissel and overwhelmed her with kisses as well, saying "Bless you, my daughter, for saving my daughter Sarah."

Zissel was especially pleased that Bathsheva had called her "my daughter." She began to think of Shlomo and tears filled her eyes.

"Sarah is an alert, intelligent child," said Zissel. "She passed the test. The whole time she was lying under the bed she didn't make a sound, even though she knew that her mother and father were nowhere nearby." Hearing herself praised so, Sarah was proud. She knew that from now on she must live up to Zissel's praise.

There had been no need to hide David as he was no longer a child. So far there had been no hunt for boys his age.

One more note must be added. When Chasidova came to the ghetto gate on her way out, the Polish guard recognized her and asked if she got her money. When she answered, "Yes, all of it," the guard looked at her suspiciously. He didn't believe it.

✳ 12 ✳ *A Question Without an Answer*

Like all the other Jewish ghettos, the ghetto of Chedalonova was surrounded by barbed wire, but this did not prevent it from becoming a gold mine for the local Polish population. Two people could carry on a conversation or pass small objects back and forth through the barbed wire, and the starving Jews of the ghetto were willing to pay high prices for anything that could be put into their mouths.

Among these starving Jews were some who had brought sizable sums of money and other valuables with them to the ghetto. Although they had lost their furniture and the merchandise in their stores, they did manage to salvage money, rings, watches, jewelry and precious gems. A brisk business developed between the Jews on one side of the barbed wire and the Poles on the other.

The Jews paid high prices for the loaves of bread and the potatoes smuggled in by the Poles. Those who had no money left could pay with a gold ring or some other piece of jewelry. Of course, a gold ring is worth far more than a loaf of bread, but the Jew knew he could not expect a Pole to have enough change to cover the difference between a loaf of bread and a gold ring. He was therefore left with the choice: He could exchange the ring for the bread or he could starve to death. If the Pole—who knew in advance what choice the Jew must make—was honest, he would give the Jew a few gold coins change, so that the Jew could buy another loaf of bread or a few more potatoes once again—but no more than once.

Although this trade was strictly forbidden and anyone caught was liable to severe punishment, both sides were willing to take the risk. Hunger for food made the Jew reckless, and hunger for gold made the Pole reckless. They learned to escape detection by the German patrols who stalked back and forth along the wire. It was possible to sneak up to the fence behind the guard's back and to cling so close to it that one could not be seen from afar.

Rozeshka had no money. She had fled from her house empty-handed and had not taken a single penny with her. Luckily for her, the generous Bathsheva did not let her starve, perhaps because of Zissel who had become almost a member of the Sharfson family. After Zissel saved Sarah, the ties between them became even stronger. Kolonymos had been one of the wealthiest men of the community, and he still had a little money left. Bathsheva "lent" some of this little to Rozeshka. Whenever she received a few gold coins from Bathsheva, Rozeshka would go over to the barbed wire fence and wait for a Pole to come selling food. The fence was only a few feet away from their house.

One day, as she approached the fence, Rozeshka let out a cry of joy. There was her friend Chasidova standing on the other side! In her joy Rozeshka forgot about the barbed wire and stretched out her hand to Chasidova. Striking the barbed wire, she cried out and withdrew her hand.

"I have been here every day for the past few days," said Chasidova, "but I could not find you."

"It's not every day that I have the money to buy food," replied Rozeshka. "We get along on very little. Each loaf of bread must last a few days."

Chasidova pushed a loaf of bread through the barbed wire, followed by a small package of butter and cheese, commenting, "This is not the most important thing. I came here to bring you something more important."

"What could be more important to a hungry person than a loaf of bread?" asked Rozeshka.

"There is something more important than bread," answered Chasidova, "there is freedom."

Hearing that, Rozeshka's eyes glittered. Chasidova had good news! A spirit of lightheartedness seized her and she asked, "How can you pass my freedom to me through the barbed wire? Once it is inside the ghetto, it will no longer be free!"

Chasidova was happy to see Rozeshka in a good mood, but she reminded her that this was not the time or place for unnecessary conversation. Looking carefully all around, she pushed a folded piece of paper through the barbed wire. "Take this. It is an identity certificate for Vanda Yagelska. With the aid of this certificate, you will be able to leave the ghetto."

"But how will I get out?" Rozeshka asked. "What can I say to the guard at the gate? What is a Polish woman doing in the ghetto?"

"You heard the story of how I got into the ghetto. You can get out the same way. There is a different guard at the gate now." Chasidova paused, then added, "I heard there was a search for the ghetto children, and many of them were snatched from their mothers' arms."

"It was horrible," answered Rozeshka. "My Zushka saved our neighbor's daughter."

"I visited the convent of Nachrovah and asked the sisters to take in a few children from the ghetto of Chedalonova in the name of Christian mercy. They told me I could bring no more than four or five girls to the convent. I don't know why they prefer girls to boys, but that's what they said. If there is anyone in the ghetto who is willing to accept this Christian charity, I will transfer the girls to safety in the convent."

Just then Chasidova looked around and saw that the German guard was approaching. Hastily she whispered, "I will come again in a week." Then she disappeared.

Rozeshka left the wire quickly, before the guard caught sight of her. Excited, she hurried home to tell Zushka all that had happened.

She could now save herself, but at a terrible price, for she would have to part from her only daughter. Heaven only knew what would be the fate of those remaining in the ghetto. Should she pay such a price to save herself?

Returning home, Rozeshka found only Bathsheva in the room. She showed her the bread and cheese and butter, and Bathsheva congratulated her on her good fortune. Rozeshka didn't know whether to tell Bathsheva about the certificate or to wait and tell her story to Zushka first. She decided not to say anything until she had heard Zushka's opinion. Rozeshka walked over to the window to see if her daughter was coming. The window overlooked Yevshova Street, but when Rozeshka looked outside, she conjured up a picture of Carolevska Street. Here, frightened, bent over Jews with burned out eyes were stumbling along the street, but on Carolevska carefree people were going about their business or strolling merrily. She was in the ghetto, but her eyes and heart were on Carolevska Street. So engrossed was Rozeshka in her daydreams that she didn't even notice Zushka walk into the house.

Zissel saw her mother standing at the window deep in thought. She walked up to her and gently put her arm on her mother's shoulder.

"Hello, mother."

Rozeshka turned around. "Oh, I didn't even see you come in. I was thinking."

"What about?" asked Zissel.

Rozeshka told her story in a whisper so low that not even Bathsheva could hear. Zissel listened and was sad. On the one hand, she wanted her mother to save herself by leaving the ghetto, for by now, it was clear that the Jews of the ghetto were all in danger of losing their lives. Who knew what the Nazis would do to them next? On the other hand, she would be left all alone, with neither father nor mother.

Zissel soon came to the conclusion that her mother must be saved, and her own personal feelings must not be allowed to interfere. Zissel herself wished to stay in the ghetto, and she had no right to hold her mother back.

"What do you think, my daughter?" asked Rozeshka.

"I think you should leave," said Zissel, "not so much because of the danger, but simply because you cannot get used to this environment. I will be fine here with the Sharfsons, and someday we will be reunited, perhaps even before the war is over."

Rozeshka sighed. "But how can I go without you? Come with me."

"No," said Zissel, "I already told Mrs. Chasidov what I think, and that is my final decision."

Mention of Chasidova reminded Rozeshka of the proposal to take girls into the convent. She told Zissel about it.

"That is very important," said Zissel. "We must tell it to the Sharfsons immediately."

Kolonymos soon came home with the children.

"This is not a story for the children to hear," decided Zissel. "We'll discuss it with the Sharfsons when we are alone."

That evening Zissel related the story while Rozeshka nodded her head in assent, for Rozeshka spoke only Polish although she understood simple Yiddish, whereas the Sharfsons spoke only Yiddish although they understood Polish. When she had finished the story, Zissel looked at the Sharfsons and asked, "What do you think of Mrs. Chasidov's proposals?"

Kolonymos began to speak, slowly and carefully. "Simple common sense dictates that anyone given the opportunity to leave the ghetto and save his own life should certainly do so. If Mrs. Blitz has the chance to get out she should go. If Zissel wants to leave, it is her right, too, but if she wants to stay behind and share the lot of the Jewish community here, she should not be prevented from this act of *kiddush haShem*. If she chooses to throw her lot in with her Jewish brethren, may she be blessed."

"What do you think of the proposal to send Sarah to the convent?" asked Bathsheva.

"That is another matter," he answered. "We must consult the *Rav* about that. It is no small thing to place a Jewish girl in Christian hands, and especially in a Catholic institution. Tomorrow I will speak with the *Rav*. This question does not only concern our Sarah'leh. It applies to all the children of the ghetto and also to those in other ghettos throughout the country."

A dismal feeling engulfed everyone in the room. Anticipation of the imminent parting made their hearts heavy. These loving souls might soon be forced to separate—perhaps forever. Their sadness was overwhelming.

The very next day, Rozeshka readied herself to leave the ghetto. "Wear one of my good dresses," offered Bathsheva. "It will take more than an identity card to fool the guard at the ghetto gate. You won't get very far in the rags worn by ghetto dwellers. If you want him to believe you are a Polish woman, you must dress properly."

Rozeshka thanked her for her generosity and "borrowed" a nice dress and an "almost new" purse. When at last Rozeshka was ready, she found that she could not leave. Her legs refused to walk through the door. Zissel stood beside her mother, unable to say a word, motioning her to go. Rozeshka, sensing her daughter's suffering, began to doubt whether she had chosen the right course of action. Finally, Bathsheva, watching the two of them, put one arm around Zissel and the other around Rozeshka and brought them close enough to embrace.

"*Nu*," she whispered, "now it is time to say good-bye.

There is no other way." Both mother and daughter began sobbing. The tears flowed from one set of eyes into the other. When they had no more strength left to cry, Zissel pulled herself up and said in a trembling voice, "Go, mother, and may God be with you."

Bathsheva kissed Rozeshka good-bye and wished her much success. Rozeshka walked over to the washbasin, washed her face again, straightened her clothing and then left the room without even glancing behind her. She was afraid that she would not have the strength to leave if she looked back at Zissel. One more glance and she would burst into tears again, and this would ruin her disguise. A Polish woman who had just collected a debt from a Jewish woman in the ghetto would not have been crying.

Secretly, Zissel followed her mother to the gate. She wanted to see with her own eyes that her mother had left the ghetto safely. Rozeshka reached the gate just after the guards had changed shifts. A new guard was standing at the gate. When Rozeshka approached him and asked for permission to leave, he looked at her in surprise and asked, "Who are you?"

Rozeshka pulled out her certificate and handed it to him. The guard looked at the certificate and asked, "What is a Polish woman doing in the Jewish ghetto?"

Rozeshka told her story about collecting a debt. The guard looked her over again, hesitating. Knowing that every second lost increased the danger, Rozeshka pretended to be insulted and began rebuking the guard.

"I am sure that neither your father nor your grandfather ever heard better Polish than mine. How can you even imagine that a ghetto Jewess could speak such Polish? Aren't you ashamed?"

Embarrassed that he himself had not thought of that, the guard bowed according to Polish custom and apologized as he opened the gate. Rozeshka walked out and headed straight for Chasidova's residence at Thirteen Milkudevska Street. Zissel returned home, her face awash with tears.

Kolonymos had left the house even before Rozeshka. He knew that she was planning to leave and he had already said good-bye and wished her much success. Then he went to speak to the *Rav*.

Listening closely as Kolonymos explained the problem, the *Rav* answered, "You are not the first person to bring up this question. For several days I have been searching for an answer." Pointing to the Rambam's *Mishneh Torah* open before him, the *Rav* continued, "I am studying the laws of *kiddush haShem* in the Rambam, but I have not yet found the answer. The girls are not being asked to convert, but placing them in a convent may lead to their eventual conversion. There is no clear-cut decision here as to whether the mere possibility of conversion overrules the *mitzvah* of saving lives. A Jew faced with forced conversion is commanded to die rather than worship false gods. The question is whether one must choose death over the *possibility* of later being forced to convert."

The *Rav* paused and then continued, "What will happen if, God forbid, we are fated to . . . , if no one remains to reclaim the children from the convent and they are simply swallowed into the Christian world? No, I cannot answer this question."

Looking at the *Rav*'s face, Kolonymos noticed how creased it had become. It was literally lined with sorrow. Kolonymos sighed and asked again, "Then what shall I do?"

The *Rav* looked down and did not answer. He *could* not answer the burning question of the hour. Kolonymos sensed his anguish and asked no more. Instead, he said, "We will take each new trouble as it comes. The child hunt is over now, and there is nothing to gain from any further discussion. Let us hope and pray that God answers our prayers and delivers us from further suffering."

"Amen," said the *Rav* as Kolonymos rose to leave.

At home, Bathsheva was waiting impatiently. There was no need for her to voice her question; it could be read in her eyes. "The *Rav* had no clear answer for us," replied Kolonymos. "Apparently this question never came up before and was not dealt with in any of the responsa."

"Then what shall we do?" asked Bathsheva.

"If there is no clear-cut prohibition involved, we must save the child," answered her husband.

Bathsheva heaved a sigh of relief. It was evident that this was what she had wished to hear.

They had one week to prepare Sarah for the parting. In one week Chasidova had promised to be at the fence again. Bathsheva enlisted Zissel's help. Sarah loved Zissel. It was she who had saved her the night of the child hunt and had told her how bright she was. Sarah was anxious for Zissel to praise her again, and she constantly tried to earn more praise. Every day, Sarah and Zissel would discuss the future. Zissel described to Sarah the good woman who would come to take her to a house in which there were other girls like herself from the ghetto, and there she would live happily for a time. Before long her father and mother would come to take her home.

Of course, continued Zissel, Sarah was still very young, but she was also very bright, and a bright girl doesn't cry even if she has to be away from her father and mother for a short time. Sarah listened to Zissel and tried to act grown up. She promised not to cry.

How would they smuggle Sarah out of the ghetto? Kolonymos checked the barbed wire fence and discovered that it was possible. The fence had been bent in one corner to enable small packages to be passed underneath it. The thin body of a ghetto child could also pass through such a space.

During those days, Shlomo's name was frequently mentioned. Shlomo had parted from them of his own free will and not through force of circumstance.

"It was God's mercy that Shlomo went to Eretz Yisrael to live there in peace, instead of remaining in Chedalonova," Kolonymos would say.

Bathsheva sighed and answered, "We haven't heard a word from him in such a long time."

"There is a war going on, and no mail comes to Germany or Poland from alien countries," replied Kolonymos.

"True," agreed Bathsheva, "but for an entire year before the war broke out we didn't receive a letter. Who knows what's happening to him?"

Zissel tried to reassure them. "People work very hard on the *kibbutz*. At night they are too tired to sit down and write letters. Once one gets in the habit of postponing letter writing from day to day, the letter never gets written."

To tell the truth, Zissel herself was quite worried by the fact that Shlomo had not written to his parents for such a long time, but she tried to reassure them—and herself—that all must be well with Shlomo.

The parting of Bathsheva and Kolonymos from their daughter Sarah was a painful one, especially for the parents, who knew that their promises of a swift reunion might only be wishful thinking. On the set date, they went to the fence. Kolonymos and Bathsheva stood back while Zissel approached the fence. A minute later she returned to say that Chasidova had arrived. Zissel and Bathsheva remained in the background while Kolonymos took Sarah's hand and walked with her to the opening. Sarah crawled on all fours through the hole. Her father helped push her through while Chasidova helped pull her out. Then, Chasidova and Sarah, their hands linked, left the site immediately. Kolonymos returned to Bathsheva and Zissel. Bathsheva was so overwhelmed with misery that she could not walk home without the help of Zissel and Kolonymos.

A few people passed them on the way, but even if there were any witnesses to Sarah's escape, there was no danger that anyone in the ghetto would report it.

✳ 13 ✳ *Birobidzhan*

No one sent Elkas's group off or wished them well as they left the Holy Land and their fellow Jews for Soviet Russia. No one knew or cared how they planned to go. Either they went by train from Damascus through Syria and Turkey, or they went by sea to Turkey and from there to Russia. In any case, they reached the small Jewish collective "Red Joy" in Birobidzhan. The few dozen families who were members of the collective gave them a warm welcome. They showed them the houses and barns and chicken coops and tried to make them comfortable.

Elka's group had seven members: Shmuel and Sheindel of Nachrovah, Aharon and Elka of Temyonovah, Shlomo of Chedalonova, Tzvi of Efesova, and Dov of Ovdanova. They had not gone to the city to become factory workers for they were all *chalutzim*, and their place was in the fields. Their first days in the collective were days of rejoicing. They were home at last. Everyone spoke Yiddish. Even the sign at the train station was in Yiddish, and of course, there was a local Yiddish newspaper, *Truth from Birobidzhan*.

Reading the newpaper for the first time, the *chalutzim* raised their eyebrows in surprise at the numerous spelling mistakes. No final letter forms were used at the end of a word. When they first noticed the funny spelling of Birobidzhan at the train station, they had shrugged their shoulders and joked, "The manager of the train station need not be a Yiddish scholar." But newspaper editors should know better. In addition, Yiddish words of Hebrew origin were spelled and pronounced strangely.

When Shlomo asked Aron, the editor of the paper, about this, he laughed and said, "It says in the *gemara* that the final letter forms were dictated by the prophets. What do we have to do with prophets? And we have divorced 'Hebrew' words from the Holy Tongue. We want nothing to do with the language of the clericals."

Shlomo understood from this that Aron, too, was a former *yeshivah* student. Little by little, the *chalutzim* got used to the strange spelling and learned to read the newspaper fluently.

There were different branches of work on the commune. Some members worked in the barns and some in the chicken coops. But most, including Elka's group, worked in the fields. Surprisingly, the field work was mechanized. Ploughing was done by a tractor, not by horses or bulls. The new members asked the veterans why their collective was luckier than all the others they had passed on the way. No one else had a tractor.

"This tractor is a present from the Jews of America," answered Borich, the head of the collective.

"What?" Shlomo was astounded. "You accepted a present from your enemies the capitalists? Why did the Jews of America donate a tractor to those who hate them?"

"We only know what we see with our own eyes," answered Borich. "Not every question can be answered, but this need not hinder our building a Socialist society."

Everyone in the collective worked from sunup to sundown, with an hour break at lunchtime. The field hands did not go home to eat. They ate their bowls of cereal in the fields, while sitting on piles of hay. The food was plentiful but the menu was monotonous. Every day they would make a small fire in a pit in the field and heat up a huge pot of cereal.

At sundown, everyone went home. "Home" for the new members was two rooms in a wooden hut where they ate supper together. Elka and Sheindel managed to cook a good meal from only a few dairy products and vegetables. The time was summer.

After long days of hard work, the new members became impatient for a day of rest. They had worked for two weeks without stopping. Tired and eager to have a day off, they were disappointed when no such day came. A month passed, and still no day off. On the *kibbutz* no one had observed Shabbath on the seventh day, but everyone was given at least one day of rest each month. Not all rested on the same day, but in the course of a month, everyone had at least one day off. Tzvi and Dov went to the director of the commune to ask for a day of rest.

"What do you want to do on that day?" asked Borich.

"Nothing," answered Tzvi and Dov. "We want one day off to do nothing. We only want to rest, to gather strength to work the next day."

"Well," answered Borich, "the Soviet constitution grants

workers one day of rest a week, and soon the workweek will be reduced to five days, unlike the capitalist countries, which take advantage of their workers six days a week. The workday will also be reduced from eight hours a day to seven, in contrast to that of capitalistic countries. However, the local party committee has requested that we volunteer to work a ten-hour workday seven days a week."

"Why?" asked Dov and Tzvi. "We are not at war and there is no state of emergency."

"I don't know why," answered Borich, "but if you like, you can ask the *politruk* when he comes on his next visit. He must surely know the answer. You can talk to him as if he were one of your group. Here in Russia, we are all friends. What could be easier or pleasanter than to talk to a friend? When he comes, I'll call you and you can ask him all the questions you asked me."

A few days later, Borich summoned Tzvi and Dov to his office. As they entered, a stranger stood up, shook their hands and greeted them warmly, "Welcome, my comrades."

Tzvi and Dov returned the greeting.

"This is our Comrade Itzik, the *politruk*," introduced Borich. "I have called you to ask Itzik everything you asked me. Please sit down."

Tzvi and Dov took their seats and repeated their questions before Itzik, adding a few new ones. Itzik sat and listened. The more they asked, the smaller his smile became until finally it disappeared altogether. It was replaced by a look of fury.

"Where do you come from?" asked Itzik when both Dov and Tzvi had finally finished.

"We come from Eretz Yisrael," they answered.

"The fascist Zionists poisoned your souls," said Itzik. "They accustomed you to unregulated criticism and planted doubts in your heads about the most obvious facts. The Socialist State cannot be built on a base of criticism, doubts and unlimited questions. Socialism is based upon discipline. Nevertheless, I will answer a few of your questions, just to prove that they can be answered.

"You asked why we accept presents from our enemies, the Jews of America. Personally, we may hate them, but we have nothing against their money. On the contrary, the money that they gained so unjustly is now being used to build the Socialist State and bring justice to the world.

"As to your question regarding volunteer work with no day of rest, this proves your misunderstanding of Socialism. We believe that man must sacrifice his own personal interests on behalf of Socialism. What value does one life have compared to the ideal of a Socialist world built on justice and integrity? There is nothing more praiseworthy than a man who volunteers to work with his last iota of strength.

"However, since not all Soviet citizens have the maturity to volunteer of their own free will, as bourgeois education has spoiled them and taught individuals to put their own needs before those of society, the Politburo and the Party have taken upon themselves to decide on our behalf how much each person must volunteer, and also to see that no one shirks his duty. This will be unnecessary once all Soviet citizens become sufficiently educated to volunteer of their own free will. The bread grown in the collectives is needed to feed the factory workers, who also work voluntarily to produce machinery for the State."

Tzvi and Dov listened but did not understand. They had always thought that Man was the supreme consideration in the U.S.S.R. All efforts were to be directed at improving the lot of the individual. Now, they had just been informed that Man must sacrifice himself, to his last ounce of strength, on behalf of the Socialist State.

But if each individual sacrificed himself, who would be left to enjoy the results? If they were all sacrifices, for whom were they sacrificing themselves? If it was all for the sake of the next generation, then each generation would have to sacrifice itself on behalf of the next until the end of all the generations—and the generation that realized that it was the last of all generations would certainly not be able to enjoy life.

Itzik looked at Tzvi and Dov and saw that his answers had not satisfied them. Angrily, he stood up and proclaimed, "We will not allow everyone to think as he pleases. We must all think alike!"

Dov dared to interrupt. "Well, then, let everyone else think just as I do, and then everyone will think alike! How can everyone tell what everyone else is thinking?"

This made Itzik's ears ring. He was a member of the Komsomol and never before in his entire life had he heard such heresy. He pounded on the table and shouted at the top of his voice, "You are counterrevolutionary! You came to the U.S.S.R. to spread fascist Zionist propaganda! Be careful, or you will get what you deserve! Now out of here!"

Borich stood in a corner, his body quaking. He feared that he would be blamed for accepting these people into the collective, knowing who they truly were. Tzvi and Dov left the room in a state of shock, unable to believe what had happened. It had all taken place so fast that they didn't yet grasp fully what had occurred. What had they said to make Itzik so angry? What was their sin? Why had he labeled them counterrevolutionary? Is anyone who asks a question because he wants to know the answer counterrevolutionary?

The news spread throughout the commune like wildfire. Everyone took Itzik's side against the new members. It was not only Borich who was afraid for his own skin. Every member of the collective was afraid that he would be punished for the sins of the new members. They knew that all over the U.S.S.R. counterrevolutionary forces were being eradicated. Anyone who had any contact with someone suspected of being disloyal to the government was in danger. Hundreds and thousands of people were disappearing nightly, and no one knew where they were. If the N.K.V.D. heard of the incident in Red Rejoicing, its members would all fall under suspicion. Even if they had not invited these new members to their commune, they should have notified the government at once of their treason. If they had not done so, they were party to the crime against the government.

One might ask how the members of Red Rejoicing could have notified the government before they themselves were aware of the treason. The answer is that in the U.S.S.R. anyone not proven innocent is assumed guilty. Even if we assume that the veterans of the commune did not report Elka's group because they were unaware of their opinions, the possibility remains that they themselves were subconsciously influenced by the foreigners. Counterrevolution is a contagious illness, and an ill or infected person does not always realize that he is sick. There was ample reason for the other members of the collective to be afraid.

From that day on, they refrained from any unnecessary contact with these newcomers who had so quickly brought ill fame to their collective. They were sure that Itzik would report his meeting to the government, and that the results would soon follow. No one spoke a word to the *chalutzim* except for their fellow workers in the fields, and then only concerning their work and only when absolutely necessary.

After Dov and Tzvi had reported their conversation with Itzik to the group, all sank into despair. In less than no time, the rosy future that they had envisioned was utterly destroyed. They had believed that here, in the Soviet Union, they would find a state that sacrificed itself for the sake of mankind. Now Itzik had informed them that it was they who must sacrifice themselves for the good of the State.

These *chalutzim* knew the Socialist dialectic inside out, and now they delved deeper and deeper, trying to find a dialectic rationale for Itzik's pronunciations, but in vain. His words had no logical basis whatsoever, and there was no satisfactory explanation for the discrepancies. Neither could the *chalutzim* make any sense of Itzik's declaration that the individual is prohibited from independent thought and must think what everyone else is thinking. How was such a thing possible?

Not only were the members of Elka's group disappointed and disillusioned with the Soviet ideology, they again found themselves at odds with society since the members of the collective ostracized them completely. They had fled from the *kibbutz* in Eretz Yisrael because they felt isolated and left out, but now they had met the same destiny in Soviet Russia.

Nevertheless, the *chalutzim* did not allow themselves to mope for long. In a few days the spirit of rebellion drove away their despair. They would show the other members of the collective that they were self-sufficient, that they had a world of their own. They began to speak Hebrew among themselves loud enough for the others to hear. As soon as a few Hebrew words were heard, all those around them would disappear, and the *chalutzim* would find themselves standing alone. No one even dared listen to them, for Hebrew was outlawed as a counterrevolutionary language. In their own cottage the group sang Hebrew songs and danced the *horah* just as they had on the *kibbutz*. It was a real state of rebellion.

No more than three days later, the members of Elka's group were summoned to the director's office. They were met by an officer of the N.K.V.D.—not a Jew this time, but a Russian. He did not shake their hands, nor did he even return their greeting. Wordlessly, he gestured to them to sit down. Borich was their translator, as they had not yet learned to speak Russian. The officer's first question was, "Who is your leader?"

"We have no leader," answered Aharon. "We are all equal."

"Well, then," asked the officer, "who brought you here?"

"We all agreed unanimously to come."

"There is always one person who speaks up first and whose ideas are adopted by the others," insisted the officer.

"I was the first to suggest that we immigrate to the U.S.S.R.," volunteered Elka.

The officer looked at her and pronounced, "If so, then you are their leader." Turning to Elka, he accused them all: "You are Zionists!"

"We *were* Zionists before we emigrated," Elka corrected him. "We came to Russia only after we ceased being Zionists."

"If so," asked the officer, "why do you continue to speak Hebrew?"

"That is the language of the Jews," answered Elka.

"No," disagreed the officer, "the Jewish language is Yiddish, as spoken here in Birobidzhan. It is not Hebrew!"

Elka had no answer. Shmuel tried to come to her defense. "It is just a question of habit. We were used to speaking Hebrew before, and we simply continue out of habit."

"It is a bad habit," cut in the officer. "It must be forcibly eradicated. You came to the U.S.S.R. to propagate Zionist propaganda and to incite other Jews to leave Birobidzhan and immigrate to Palestine. We know exactly who you are. You cannot fool us. We have no faith in Hebrews." (The word "Jew" had been outlawed in the U.S.S.R.).

Looking at Borich, he continued, "Except for a few, you are all traitors. You cause trouble throughout the entire world."

Shlomo, listening to Borich translate this conversation into Yiddish, wondered to himself, "How can a Jew listen tranquilly to such words? Doesn't he realize how he is being degraded?"

Looking into Borich's eyes, Shlomo suddenly realized that he was actually enjoying the conversation.

"This Borich has the soul of a slave," thought Shlomo. "Even while his ear is being pierced he continues to declare, 'I love my master and don't want to be free.' This Russian's comments would pierce the ears of any free Jew, but Borich is not even aware that he is being humiliated. He loves his master too much."

Shlomo could no longer remain silent. "I fled from the Gentiles who hate Jews to come here," he said, "because I thought that there was no anti-Semitism in Russia. Now I see that you, too, hate Jews."

The official coolly corrected him, "Here there is no anti-Semitism. You are simply traitors who must be reeducated. Those who cooperate with us in their reeducation may later become productive members of society and play a role in spreading Socialism throughout the world."

The minute of silence that followed seemed to last a thousand years. Then the officer continued, "You must confess the truth—that you came to the U.S.S.R. to disseminate Zionist propaganda and to incite Jews to emigrate from Birobidzhan to Palestine."

"That is not true," protested Shlomo. "We have nothing to confess."

"Only we know the truth," answered the official.

"No one can truly know what anyone is thinking but he himself," persisted Shlomo.

"There can be only one truth, not two," countered the official. "That you must admit."

"Yes," agreed Shlomo. "That I admit."

"Well, then," continued the official, "we are the sole possessors of that one single truth. If you disagree with us, then you cannot claim to be speaking the truth. Can there be any other truth? You Hebrews love to study the Talmud, and the Talmud teaches you all kinds of twisted logic, but you will not succeed in fooling us. We know you better than you know yourselves."

Shlomo was stung by this reference to the Talmud. He turned in his seat as though bitten by a snake. Fortunately he was able to control himself. He pressed his lips together, stifling his opinion of the Soviet government.

The officer continued, "You may now go home and begin packing. This afternoon you will be transported to your new places."

The seven rose and left the room without so much as a word of parting to the Russian. Why should they wish the official well if he would not respond in kind? On their way home they didn't meet a single member of the commune. It was as if no one else lived there any more. They had no idea where they were being taken, but they were reasonably sure that it would not be a paradise.

Two hours later a car came and transported Elka's group from the collective to the train station. For the last time they read the funny Yiddish spelling of Birobidzhan. They were loaded on freight trains, not passenger coaches, each individual in a separate car. Apparently the group was to be split up. Nevertheless, they were not alone. Each car was packed to capacity. Many people in the U.S.S.R. must be in need of reeducation, and the government had undertaken to supply it to all free of charge.

Elka did not board the train. Two N.K.V.D. officers escorted her somewhere on foot. Apparently the leader of the group was accorded special treatment.

After a long, tiring trip, part by train and part on foot, with only bread and water to sustain him, Shlomo arrived at his destination, a forced labor camp.

Elka's group was fortunate in that they were not first brought before a police investigator. Perhaps all the investigators were too busy that day to be able to devote any time to them. It was really just as well, for they would only have ended up in the same place after the investigation and the torture.

✶ 14 ✶ *Zissel Leaves the Ghetto*

People were very surprised when Rozeshka left Zissel behind in the ghetto, but Zissel's strength of character was even more surprising. She was prepared to forgo her own salvation and to share the destiny of the other Jews of Chedalonova, an act worthy of a true spiritual leader. People of this caliber were desperately needed to provide guidance and support at such a troubled time. But what motivation could bring a young girl, in no public position of leadership, to disregard her own personal interest and share in the common misfortune?

Rozeshka's behavior, on the other hand, was considered appalling. What kind of a mother deserts her daughter to save her own skin? One can understand the opposite situation, such as Bathsheva helping her daughter Sarah leave the ghetto. But the sight of a mother leaving her own daughter behind while the mother herself leaves for safety was quite singular. It is an unusual mother who thinks only of herself and forsakes her daughter instead of sharing her fate, even if she is unable to help her in any way.

The truth was that both Zissel and Rozeshka had good reasons for what they did. Two things prevented Zissel from leaving the ghetto. First of all, she still felt that her fate was bound up with Shlomo, and she could not bring herself to forsake his parents. What would Shlomo say about such an act? A daughter would not desert her own father and mother, and Zissel, who felt as though Bathsheva and Kolonymos were her parents, could not leave them. A small child like Sarah could leave her parents behind, but not a young woman of twenty.

There was a second reason. Once the Jews realized that the forced deportations terminated in death, the ghetto youth had united and were organizing mass resistance to their German oppressors. They were not willing to let the Nazis take their lives without paying a high price. They would wait until it was clear that all hope was gone, but then they would revolt and oppose the Nazis with force. At least they would die honorably. They might not be able to save their own lives, but at least they could save their honor and the honor of the Jewish people.

Zissel, having lived in Eretz Yisrael, felt even more responsible for the honor of Israel. How could she, who had immigrated to Eretz Yisrael because of the abuse her people suffered in the diaspora, desert the youth now when they had all united to save Israel's honor? Were she now to leave the ghetto in the guise of a Pole, she would be a traitor, both in her own eyes and in those of her friends.

Rozeshka, on the other hand, had ample reason to leave, even though it meant leaving her daughter Zushka behind. She knew that Zissel would be loyal to the Sharfsons and to the other young people of the ghetto. Nevertheless she did not lose hope. She knew how worried the Sharfsons were about their daughter Sarah in the convent in Nachrovah. Their fear that she would forget her Judaism kept them awake at night. She would wait until their fear had become almost unbearable, and then she would suggest that they send Zushka out of the ghetto so that she could visit Sarah in the convent and remind her that she was Jewish. Had Rozeshka remained in the ghetto, Zushka would never have consented to leave her mother. But now that Rozeshka had left, perhaps Zushka too would consent to leave—not in order to save her own life, but to save Sarah, who was so deeply attached to her.

As mistaken as Rozeshka was in her desire to be a Pole and not a Jew, she was not in the least mistaken regarding the surest way to draw Zushka out of the ghetto. She herself was settled in Chasidova's home, but all her thoughts revolved around her daughter. Every day that Zushka remained in the ghetto seemed like a thousand years. Nevertheless, Rozeshka held herself back, waiting for the critical moment.

Before Chasidova had smuggled Sarah out through the fence, she had spoken with Zissel and promised to return to the fence once each week to bring Zissel regards from her mother. These meetings were quite dangerous and could not be held more often, but they would suffice to keep mother and daughter in touch with each other. Great care was needed that neither Germans nor Poles notice Chasidova at the fence. Most Poles, unlike Chasidova, were in the service of the Angel of Death. Zissel was fully aware of this and was very worried about her mother. The very sight of Chasidova on the other side of the barbed wire was sufficient to quiet her fears. She knew that if, God forbid, something happened to her mother, Chasidova would not come to the fence. Not only would she not come to bring her bad news about Rozeshka, she herself would be the subject of bad news. Any Gentile caught hiding a Jew was liable to the death penalty.

But Zissel was not satisfied with seeing Chasidova standing beside the fence. She wanted to hear in detail how her mother was faring. The messages exchanged across the fence were like telegrams—short and meaningful. There was no time for lengthy conversation.

"Your mother wants you to watch over Sarah in the convent and keep her from forgetting her Judaism," said Chasidova.

"How can I watch over her if I am in the ghetto and she is in the convent?" asked Sarah, wondering why her mother was suddenly so concerned for Sarah's Jewish identity.

"You must leave the ghetto and come to us," replied Chasidova, "so that you can watch over Sarah. She is very attached to you. And only you will be able to get her out of the convent when no one else is left."

It was clear what Chasidova meant. The lives of the Jews in the ghetto were in danger. Zissel realized that her mother's primary concern was not over Sarah, but for her.

Just then Chasidova noticed that the German guard had reached the end of the street and was about to turn around and start walking back toward them. She disappeared at once, leaving behind a stunned Zissel. Even if her mother's main concern was for her, she was right about Sarah. When the day came for her to leave the ghetto, there might be no one left to claim her.

Zissel went home to talk to Bathsheva. As she told her story, she looked into Bathsheva's eyes, trying to read her thoughts. Bathsheva's eyes lit up with joy as she listened to the proposal.

"A blessing on your mother and Chasidova!" she said. "There are still good people left in this world—people who are still faithful to each other."

Just then the door opened and Kolonymos stood in the doorway. Bathsheva didn't even wait for him to enter the room before blurting out, "Did you hear, Kolonymos, what Zissel said?"

"How could I hear what she said before I was home?" asked Kolonymos. Bathsheva quickly told him Zissel's story.

"That is worth hearing," said Kolonymos. "Zissel, you must accept this offer. You will be able to work for a Jewish cause outside the ghetto as well as inside. Since we sent Sarah away a week ago, I have not been able to sleep at night. I am afraid that she will forget who she is and will not return to her people. The *Rav* did not forbid me to send her to the convent, but neither did he tell me that it was permissible. Sarah is in grave danger. This offer has given me a ray of hope. No matter what happens to those of us here in the ghetto, there will be someone to claim Sarah from the convent when the day comes."

Listening to Kolonymos, Zissel thought to herself, "Although I didn't repeat Chasidova's dire warning, Kolonymos is thinking along exactly the same lines. I spoke only of watching over Sarah until her mother and father came to get her, but Kolonymos spoke of the possibility that no one else would be left."

This convinced Zissel that she would not be betraying the Sharfsons by leaving. On the contrary, she would be fulfilling their request. Neither would she be betraying her friends, as she was not running away to save herself, but rather going to protect a Jewish child.

When Kolonymos saw that Zissel had taken his words to heart, he added, "Sarah cannot be the only ghetto child in the convent. There must be other Jewish girls with her. You, Zissel, must watch over them all. You have been chosen to fulfill an important task. I pray that you will succeed."

Kolonymos spoke fervently, as though this were a prophesy for Zissel. But then Kolonymos became very thoughtful. "We have been talking as though Zissel can simply walk out of the ghetto. We've forgotten that she can't get out even if she wants to!"

"There is a way to get out," replied Zissel, "if I receive permission from my friends."

"Then by all means, consult with your friends," agreed Kolonymos. "You cannot just leave them, but explain to them that your mission is to preserve Jewish lives on behalf of the Jewish people."

Zissel's friends had organized a group to resist the Nazis with force and they were in desperate need of weapons. There was an organization called the Polish Riflemen composed of young, armed Poles who also opposed the Germans. The Jewish youth fully realized that most Poles hated Jews no less than the Germans did, but they hoped that the Riflemen would agree to supply them with weapons to fight their common enemy.

Searching for a way to contact the Polish Riflemen, the

Jewish youth had discovered an underground sewage system connecting Yevshova Street in the ghetto with Carolevska Street outside the ghetto. One had to walk underground, through the sewage pipes, for a few blocks to Carolevska Street. If one of the Riflemen was on guard there, he would remove the cover of the sewage pipe when the street was empty, and the messenger could climb out onto the street. Chasidova had relayed a message from the Jewish youth to the Riflemen, who had then sent a guard to Carolevska Street. Menachem, who looked just like a Pole, was the messenger. He was not usually too successful in his mission, but something is better than nothing. It took several "strolls" through the sewage pipes before he succeeded in acquiring a few pistols that could be concealed under his clothing. Zissel had heard of this passageway. If she received permission from the group, she would accompany Menachem on his next venture.

That very day, Zissel approached Mordechai, the leader of the group. Mordechai insisted that her request be put to a vote, and the following day at their general meeting, Mordechai told the group of Zissel's plan and asked for their opinions. Some were opposed on the grounds that Zissel could only save individuals, whereas the ghetto uprising would redeem the honor of the whole Jewish people and so should take precedence. Others said that it was better to save Jewish lives rather than Jewish honor. Once all hope was gone, they would try to save their honor, but so long as there was a possibility of saving even a small number of lives, this certainly took precedence. At the final vote, it was decided to allow Zissel to leave the ghetto.

When Zissel returned home and told the Sharfsons, they sighed with relief. "How will you get out?" Kolonymos asked.

"I can't tell you," answered Zissel, "but there is a way."

At Chasidova's next visit to the fence, Zissel told her of her decision to leave the ghetto. With great joy, Chasidova promised, "I will prepare a place for you to hide. It is not advisable for two Jewesses to live together. Also, you'll want to visit the convent in Nachrovah, so it's safer for you to live there. It will save unnecessary train trips. Even with a Polish identity card it is dangerous for you to walk outside too much. You can easily pass for a Pole, but nevertheless there are evil people nowadays who are on the lookout for Jews everywhere. I have already spoken to my brother-in-law in Nachrovah, and they have agreed to take you into their house, which is not very far from the convent. We will have an identity card prepared for you. When you get out of the ghetto, you will come to my house to see your mother, and then my husband will accompany you to his brother's house in Nachrovah." Before the guard reached the end of the street, the two women had ended their conversation and said good-bye.

A few days later Zissel, bearing an identity card with the name Zushka Yosefova, left the ghetto and moved into the Chasidov home in Nachrovah.

✱ 15 ✱ *Zissel Visits Sarah*

There were no children in the Chasidov family of Nachrovah, only a husband and wife. He was a postal clerk and she a housewife. They received Zissel warmly and a bit apologetically, as they were fully aware of Polish complicity in the solution to the Jewish problem. They had heard from their brother-in-law of the death of Zissel's father and they were ashamed of their Polish brethren. Mr. and Mrs. Chasidov tried to make up all these wrongs to Zissel and to lighten her loneliness as much as they could.

Their house consisted of three rooms plus a kitchen and washroom, each room leading to the next. The house itself stood a bit apart from the neighbors' and there were few visitors. Zissel stayed inside, not going out unless it was absolutely necessary. Her mother Rozeshka had no reason to leave the house at all, but Zissel had left the ghetto to visit Sarah.

The house was not far from the convent, but when Zissel counted the streets she would have to cross to reach the convent, her heart began to pound. She had a Polish identity certificate stating that she was Zushka Yosefova from Chedalonova, and she looked Polish. Still, she must be extremely careful. The Poles were suspicious of all new faces. They knew that the Jews could not be trusted and were likely to masquerade as Poles, and they had already caught a few doing it. The sly, devious Jews would use any means possible to deceive the government, and the Poles checked all suspects carefully.

Chasidova helped Zissel get ready to visit the convent. She said, "First and foremost, you must stand up straight, put a smile on your face and a bit of mischief in your eyes, and look all passerbys straight in the eye, without looking down. In short, you must walk lightheartedly and with self-confidence, as if to say, 'The whole world was created only for my sake.' "

As she listened to Chasidova's speech, Zissel became increasingly worried and nervous. When Chasidova saw her agitation, she asked, "Why are you so upset, my daughter? We are all alone now. There are no strangers in the house."

"After hearing your description of how I must appear, I am afraid that I will not succeed," said Zissel.

"Don't worry," Chasidova reassured her. "There is no more dangerous enemy than worry itself. Worry is the father of all fear and the mother of all misfortune."

Zissel sighed and said, "How can I drive worry away? Did worry ask permission to enter my heart? No, it broke in like a thief and cannot be driven out."

Chasidova, seeing how tired and depressed Zissel was, said, "Lie down and rest for a while, my daughter. You will wake up with renewed strength, and your self-confidence will return."

Zissel went back to her room, lay down on the sofa and

immediately fell asleep. When she woke up two hours later, she felt much better. Walking over to the mirror, she examined her appearance. She stood up straight, put a smile on her face, and tried to look confident and nonchalant. She was satisfied that she could indeed pass for a Pole. She walked back and forth in front of the mirror, watching her own bearing. It made her happy to see that she was quite successful. She looked like a young woman with a rosy future— the whole world open before her.

There was only one detail that interfered with the picture—her eyes. The long months in the ghetto had cast sadness in her eyes—day by day, hour by hour. Now this sadness could not be erased. If she tried to force her eyes to smile, her face looked so distorted that it made a mockery of her. To smile with your lips was simple, but to put joy in your eyes, there must be joy in your soul as well. There could be no greater enemy at a time like this than Zissel's eyes.

Zissel began to despair. After one more look in the mirror, she burst into tears. Hearing Zissel cry, Chasidova came to see what had happened. She looked at Zissel and was stunned. All the suffering of the whole world was mirrored in Zissel's eyes just then.

"Why, you need sunglasses," suggested Chasidova. "The sun outside is blinding, and sunglasses can be very helpful."

Zissel stopped crying, and a smile spread across her face. She hugged Chasidova and said, "If there are still women like you in this world, there is no cause for despair."

Chasidova stroked Zissel's head and answered, "A girl your age should not be talking about despair."

In the evening, when Mr. Chasidov came home, Zissel

asked him what news he had heard. Every day she asked the same question. She knew that if there was bad news, he would not tell her; nevertheless she had not given up hope of hearing good news. So far, his answer had always been that there was nothing really new, and his answer that evening was no different.

In truth, there had been very bad news that day, but Mr. Chasidov did not disclose it. He had heard in town that there had been another roundup of ghetto Jews in Chedalonova, but he could not bring himself to tell Zissel. At night, after she was asleep, Mrs. Chasidov told her husband of Zissel's session before the mirror. Her husband sighed and said, "Poor girl. The world has gone crazy. Millions of people have forgotten all their desires and have only one passion in life—to murder Jews." Then he told his wife what he had heard in town.

The next day, Zissel visited the convent, her certificate in her purse and sunglasses on her face. She walked upright, perhaps even a bit too upright. Her gait was gay, almost dancing, her feet barely touching the ground. In the convent she introduced herself as a friend of the Sharfson family who had come to visit Sarah at her parents' request. Maria, the head nun, was not too enthusiastic about the visit, but she did not turn her guest away.

"I will call Sarah and you may see her," said Maria.

"I want to speak to Sarah privately. The child will be too shy to talk about her parents in public," said Zissel.

Maria hesitated for a minute, then gave her consent. "Very well, you may wait in this room and I'll send Sarah in to you."

She motioned to a room on the left. Zissel thanked Maria and went into the room to wait.

When Sarah entered and first caught sight of Zissel, her eyes filled with tears. Had she not suddenly remembered that bright, intelligent girls don't cry, she would have burst out crying. Zissel kissed her warmly and began to speak of her parents.

"How is David? Were any more Jews taken away from the ghetto?" asked Sarah.

"No," answered Zissel. "There have been no more man-hunts and there will be no more. David misses you as much as you miss him. But soon your mother and father will come to take you home and you and David will be together again.

"Now I must go," Zissel continued, "but I promise to come and visit you again soon."

Then she added, "If Maria asks you how you know me and what my name is, tell her that we were friends at home, not in the ghetto, and that my name is Zushka. You are a clever girl and I can depend on you to remember. After all, Zissel and Zushka sound very much alike, don't they?"

She nodded her head. She did not want to remain in the convent by herself, but Zissel had reminded her again that she was smart, and she knew that now was not the time to cry. With great effort she held back her tears.

Zissel held Sarah's hand as they left the room together. She managed to ask Sarah one more question: Were there other Jewish girls from the ghetto with her in the convent?

"Yes," answered Sarah, "there are five—Rivkah, Cha-vah, Rachel, Leah, and Brachah. They are also from the ghetto." Withdrawing her hand from Zissel's, she pointed toward the yard, saying, "Now they are playing outside. I was playing with them before Maria called me in."

Zissel bent over and kissed Sarah, and the two of them left the room together. "Go back to your games and your friends," said Zissel. "I will come again soon."

Maria was waiting for them in the hall. Zissel offered Maria her hand and said, "Good-bye. I am very happy to see that Sarah is very comfortable here."

Maria shook Zissel's hand, took a long look at her, and asked, "Do you live here in Nachrovah?"

"No," answered Zissel, "I'm from Chedalonova. I come to Nachrovah from time to time to visit my relatives here."

"It is not advisable to visit these ghetto children too often," said Maria. "We are taking great risks on their behalf and cannot be too careful."

"Of course, I understand," agreed Zissel. "I have no intention of coming often. I shall leave long intervals between my visits." She tried to speak calmly, nonchalantly.

During this conversation, Maria's eyes had remained fixed on Zissel. Now two other nuns, Tzorerkeh and Sinavkeh, entered the room, walked over to Maria and stood beside her. They stared silently at Zissel as she said good-bye to Maria.

Once outside the convent, Zissel began to review all that had taken place—Maria's conversation and the nuns' stares, and she realized that she had succeeded in fooling no one. Nevertheless, she was not afraid of being reported to the Germans. First of all, the nuns were not allowed to hide ghetto children either, and if they reported her, they themselves would be found out. Secondly, anyone who preached

Christian charity and was willing to save the lives of Jewish children would not knowingly cause the death of a Jewess by reporting her. True, the nuns were primarily interested in providing spiritual, not physical salvation, but they would not take responsibility for another's death. Zissel did not allow herself to worry over their reaction. She returned home, happy to have seen Sarah.

✱ 16 ✱ *Rozeshka's Death*

At first, Rozeshka was extremely cautious. Not only wouldn't she walk out of the house, she wouldn't even look out of the window. She had brought the fear she had acquired in the ghetto with her to Chasidova's house. Before, all her thoughts had been concentrated on the dangers involved in escaping from the ghetto. Perhaps she would fail to fool the guard at the gate; perhaps one of the passersby outside the ghetto would recognize her. After all, they had lived in Chedalonova for many years. Her husband had been a prominent lawyer and she, too, was well known. When Rozeshka first walked into Chasidova's house, Chasidova was shocked by her appearance. Rozeshka was pale as a sheet and her eyes glistened with fear.

"What happened?" Chasidova had asked.

"Nothing," Rozeshka had answered. "The fear alone is enough to kill me."

"Your fear is very healthy," Chasidova had remarked. "If it keeps you from becoming careless, it will keep you alive."

The Chasidov family of Chedalonova consisted of husband, wife and son. Both husband and wife were teachers, and their son was a member of the Polish Riflemen. As teachers were held in high esteem in Polish society, the neighbors did not enter their house freely. Educated people were regarded with awe and were not expected to mix freely with the lower classes. Days would pass without anyone coming to the house. When someone did call, he would not stay long. The Chasidov house was therefore an ideal place to hide. Had she not become careless, Rozeshka could have lived there for months without being noticed.

When Rozeshka heard that Zissel had reached Nachrovah safely and had even managed to visit the convent successfully, she began to regain her self-confidence. The desire grew within her to return to her old house and check that all was in order.

"The time has come for me to visit my own house," she announced one day.

"I was there already," said Chasidova. "The door is locked and you will not be able to get in. It is not at all advisable for you to go near there. You must be careful not to be seen."

"The locked door won't stop me," answered Rozeshka. "I have an extra key that I took with me when I left the house. As far as caution goes, I shall be as cautious as possible."

"There is nothing that you can do about the house," said Chasidova. "What good will it do you to visit there? No matter what condition the house is in, you will only be able to look around. Why endanger yourself just to satisfy your curiosity?"

"It is not mere idle curiosity," Rozeshka explained; "it is a very serious matter. My valuables are hidden in a secret hiding place in the house. Lately, many deserted houses have been broken into. If my house is broken into, all my late husband's and my own life savings may be stolen."

Chasidova continued to object. "How can you take precautions? All your old neighbors will recognize you."

"Clothes make the woman," answered Rozeshka. "I can change the way I walk and the way I look. After all, I only want to do this once. I have faith in my destiny. So far both Zissel and I have managed to escape safely from the ghetto. Apparently we are lucky. There is no need to be overly cautious. It would be a terrible shame if our savings were lost."

Chasidova realized that she could not dissuade Rozeshka. She did not want to be held responsible if Rozeshka were really to lose her money, and so she was silent, even though the venture could endanger her, too. If, God forbid, Rozeshka were caught, not only Chasidova, but also her husband and son, were liable to pay with their lives for having hidden her. Nevertheless, Chasidova allowed Rozeshka's material interests to take preference over her own safety.

"Many families live in that apartment building," Rozeshka assured her. "People are always coming and going. No one will even notice me."

"Well, if you have made up your mind to go, I can only pray that the Lord watch over you and keep you from all evil," said Chasidova.

"Amen," answered Rozeshka.

Chasidova helped Rozeshka prepare her disguise. Clever use of clothing and makeup can do wonders. Rozeshka managed to make herself appear much older than she had been when she left her house in Chedalonova. She walked slowly, stooped over, not in the least resembling the Rozeshka her neighbors had known. When they were finished, Chasidova looked her over and said, "For one visit, it's good enough."

Rozeshka walked over to the mirror, looked herself over, and smiled. She was pleased with her disguise.

As she left, Chasidova again wished her much success. Once outside, Rozeshka tried to attract as little attention as possible. She did not walk down the main streets, but through the alleyways. When she first caught sight of her old house, her heart began to pound. Soon she stood in the hallway, just outside the entrance to her old home. Her hands shaking, she touched the doorknob and saw that the door was locked. Rozeshka opened her purse and took out her key. She put it in the keyhole, but could not turn the lock. Over and over she tried, unsuccessfully, to open the door. Suddenly the door opened from the inside. A young man stood in the doorway.

Surprised, he looked at Rozeshka and asked, "Who are you?"

Rozeshka managed to keep her wits about her, and croaked feebly, "Have you a handout for an old lady?"

"Beggars wait for the door to be opened," answered Vlachek. "Someone who tries to open the door of a strange house himself is called a thief, not a beggar."

Rozeshka stood there, the key in her hand, not knowing what to say.

"Thieves must be brought to the police," continued Vlachek.

Frightened, Rozeshka protested, "I am no thief. This was once my own house."

"Why, this house used to belong to Jews. How can you claim that it was yours?" asked Vlachek.

At that, Rozeshka burst into tears.

Vlachek's parents came to the door. They didn't know what to make of the strange scene before them—an elderly woman standing in the hall and crying and an angry Vlachek blocking her entrance. When Vlachek told them what had happened, his mother walked over to Rozeshka, looked at her closely, and exclaimed, "Why, this is Mrs. Blitz!

"What are you doing outside of the ghetto?" she asked Rozeshka. "Aren't all the Jews in the ghetto?"

"We must turn her over to the authorities immediately," said Vlacheck. "According to the law, any Pole who does not report a Jew found outside the ghetto is liable to pay with his life."

Rozeshka cried and begged for mercy, promising to go away, and never come back.

"Well, we must think this over," said the Polish woman.

Vlacheck stood at the door, guarding Rozeshka, while his parents went inside to decide what to do with the Jewess on their doorstep.

"If we let her go now," said Vlachek's mother, "she may remain alive after the Jews in the ghetto have all been killed, and then she may come back here and claim the house. We cannot take such a chance. We will only be able to sleep in peace, confident that this house is truly ours, if we report her to the authorities."

Vlachek's father agreed. "You are right. We Poles cannot

afford to risk our property for the sake of a Jewess. They brought their troubles upon themselves. Since Jesus cursed them, they are not deserving of our mercy. This house is ours and we must make sure that Mrs. Blitz can never come here again."

It took only a few minutes for Vlachek's parents to reach their decision, but to Rozeshka it seemed like ages. Vlachek's mother returned to the door and said to her son, "You are right. We may not transgress the law."

Vlachek walked out of the house, took Rozeshka's arm, and set out for the ghetto. On the way, Rozeshka tried in her best Polish to win Vlachek over, but to no avail. To Vlachek one Jewess was just like any other. Her superb command of the Polish language made absolutely no impression on him.

As they approached the ghetto, they saw a chaotic scene before them. A bunch of bent over people were clustered before the gate, two German overseers in charge of them. Over and over, the overseers would question each member of the group and mark something down in their notebooks. Vlachek headed for the gate, Rozeshka still trying feebly to resist as he headed for the officer in charge. Just then one of the soldiers caught sight of Rozeshka, lifted the butt of his rifle and came down hard on her back, screaming at her, "It's all your fault that we are stuck here, unable to finish counting. Why did you run away?"

Vlachek turned to the soldier to tell him his story, but at that moment, the second soldier opened the gate to the ghetto and his comrade pushed everyone inside, making sure that Rozeshka received a few extra blows. The gate was closed, and Vlachek was left standing all by himself outside the ghetto. With no one there to listen to his story, he turned around and went home.

These unfortunate people were the last survivors of the ghetto of Ovdanova. So few people had remained alive that the Nazis decided it was not worthwhile to keep the ghetto there any longer. The few remaining Jews were transferred to Chedalonova, which had not yet been liquidated. On the way, one Jewess managed to escape. This caused much delay and confusion, as the German overseers could not hand over the full quota of Jews assigned to them. They counted over and over again, hoping that there had been some mistake and that the missing woman would turn up, but to no avail. They were one person short. Now that the missing Jewess had turned up, they were so grateful that they did not even vent their anger on her, contenting themselves with one good blow on her back and a few punches in the ribs as she joined the group being pushed into the ghetto.

When she saw Rozeshka standing once again in the doorway, Bathsheva was shocked beyond belief. She jumped up and cried in dismay, "Can my eyes be deceiving me? Can it really be you? Why did you come back to the ghetto?"

Rozeshka remained standing in the doorway, perfectly silent and motionless. Bathsheva was surprised that she made no response. Perhaps Mrs. Blitz was tired or ill.

"Come in and sit down, Mrs. Blitz. After a little rest you'll feel better," she offered.

But Rozeshka remained standing in the doorway, motionless. Kolonymos got up and walked over to her. He looked into Rozeshka's eyes and then said quietly to his wife, "Mrs. Blitz is no longer in this world. She doesn't even hear what you are saying to her."

Bathsheva, too, looked into Rozeshka's eyes and saw no sign of life in them. Her eyes looked as if they were made of glass. Kolonymos told his wife, "She is in shock. Something terrible must have happened to her. All we can do is put her to bed and pray that time will heal her wounds."

Bathsheva took Rozeshka by the hand and led her to her old bed, which had been empty since she had left the ghetto. She removed her coat and shoes and helped Rozeshka lie down. Rozeshka did not even blink her eyes in response. She let Bathsheva do whatever she wished.

"Poor woman," said Kolonymos, "she is completely cut off from the world around her and from her own self. She must have gone mad."

"She would never have returned to the ghetto if she were in her right mind," answered Bathsheva.

"Perhaps she was forcibly returned."

Bathsheva tried repeatedly to elicit some response from Rozeshka. She sat beside her on the bed, trying everything possible to comfort her and draw her out from the depths of her despair, but to no avail. Rozeshka did not move. Had she not continued to breathe, she might have been taken for dead. Discouraged, Bathsheva left her by herself.

That very evening the ghetto was surrounded by the S.S. Rumors flew that there would be another roundup. People began running to and fro, frantically but vainly searching for a place to hide. Soon deafening screams were heard. The raucous shouts of the S.S. mixed with the broken cries of the deportees and added to the trauma. Altogether, about one hundred men and women were deported.

The truth must be told. Under Mordechai's leadership, the Jewish youth did try to defend themselves and resist the roundup with force. Pistols in hand, they positioned themselves on the rooftop of one of the houses near the gate. Unfortunately, their pistols did not function. Only two of the youths managed to shoot one bullet apiece. Either the Polish Riflemen had purposely deceived the Jews and sent them defective weapons, or else they simply had nothing better to offer. The Nazis immediately surrounded the house and arrested the youths. Two of them were shot immediately in return for the two shots they fired, and the others were taken with the rest of the Jews to the trucks that would transport them to the trains and to Auschwitz.

When the Nazis entered the Sharfsons' room, they herded Bathsheva, Kolonymos and David to the truck, shouting at Rozeshka to get up and follow them. When she did not respond, one of the Nazi soldiers walked over to her, took a good look and saw that she was not sane. He pointed his rifle at her head and remarked, "This is a mercy killing!"

"I didn't know you were merciful to Jews!" remarked his friend.

"I am willing to do anything to kill a Jew—even to be merciful," he answered.

A shot was heard and the bullet penetrated Rozeshka's head. The Nazis herded the Sharfson family into the truck downstairs.

Bathsheva's eyes were blinded by tears. But Kolonymos pronounced the verse from Koheleth, "I praise the dead, who have already died . . ."

✱ 17 ✱ *En Route to Auschwitz*

The Jews who had been rounded up in the ghetto were crammed into two freight cars. The Sharfsons found themselves in the same car as the *Rav*, while the youths who had tried to shoot the Germans were divided between the two cars.

The Jews were not simply crammed into the freight cars. It would be more correct to say that they were thrown—or even beaten—in. Those who did not move as fast as the sound of the Nazi orders were "helped" along with murderous blows.

Inside, the situation was intolerable. There was no air, and no room to sit down. There was barely enough space for each person to stand on his own two feet. People were so packed together that no one could know for sure which were his own hands and legs and which belonged to his neighbors. Yet even in such desperate conditions, the Jews did their best to lighten the suffering of their aged *Rav*. Each person squeezed himself a bit closer to his neighbor, one person almost inside the other, until they succeeded in clearing a small space for the *Rav*, whose legs could no longer hold him up, to sit down.

Touched by their efforts, the *Rav* said, "Do not bother, my children. It is not permitted for a rabbi to cause his congregation so much trouble. Once I was young, but now I am old. My long life is over. Now we must worry about the young and try to help them find a way to remain alive. We old people will sanctify God's name through our death. We will meet death standing upright, proud to be Jews. Our youth, however, must sanctify God's name by remaining alive and by doing everything in their power to defeat the forces of evil."

Not a sound, not a sigh was heard in the car. The passengers were comforted by the words of their *Rav*, by the fact that he considered them martyrs. No one, not even the Nazis, could deny them this. On the contrary, the greater their suffering, the more they earned the title.

Peretz the *chalutz* and Mordechai were in the car with the *Rav*. As Peretz listened to the *Rav*'s speech, an idea began pounding away in his mind. Why not try to escape? The *Rav* had just charged the youth with trying to frustrate the Nazis' evil designs. In normal times, Peretz had not been one of the *Rav*'s disciples. Nor had he been a student of the *Beith Midrash*. But now that he heard the *Rav* decree that the youth must sanctify God's name by remaining alive and defeating the forces of evil—just as he and his friends had tried to do—there was not really any basic difference of opinion between them.

"Did you hear what the *Rav* said?" whispered Peretz to Mordechai.

"I heard," answered Mordechai, "but what good are speeches now?"

"The *Rav* spoke about action, not speeches," said Peretz.

"What action?"

"We must try to stay alive!"

"Is that up to us?"

"Perhaps."

"How?"

"We must try to escape this train."

Mordechai looked hard at Peretz and then said, "It's worth a try. We have nothing to lose."

"We can push a plank out of the side of the car, and when the train slows down around a turn, we'll jump. We have at least a fifty-fifty chance to save our lives. If we don't jump, we have no chance whatsoever. No one escapes from Auschwitz."

"You can't pull out a plank with bare hands," said Mordechai.

Peretz searched the freight car with his eyes. Suddenly they lit up. "I found it!" he cried.

Everyone near him turned around in surprise, not understanding what he could have found to make him so happy on the way to Auschwitz.

"What did you find?" asked Mordechai.

Peretz pointed toward the door. A metal ring, connected to a long iron bar, was screwed into the wall next to the door. The function of this bar was obvious. In normal times this had been a freight car used to transport herds of cattle. As cows were expensive, great care was taken not to damage the herds in any way en route. The Jews on their way to Auschwitz could be transported in stuffy, airless cars; but not the cows. While transporting cows, the car door was opened and the iron bar put across the doorway to keep the cattle from falling out. The cows could then stand safely beside the open door and breathe fresh air on their trip. Now that the Nazis had locked the door from the outside, the bar was useless and had been hung on a hook at the top of the wall. It reached down almost to the floor.

Peretz and Mordechai lost no time. They pushed themselves over to the bar and tried to free the hook from the wall. This was no easy job. It had been screwed to the wall years ago and was all rusty, but the combination of youth, muscles, and above all, the will to live, forced the hook to surrender. The bar was in their hands.

Now the work was just beginning. They would have to bang a hole in the wall, which would make a lot of noise. Nevertheless, there was no danger that the Nazis in the last car would hear them above the din made by the train itself. Peretz and Mordechai took turns and finally succeeded in breaking through the wall.

Now they had to widen the hole. This was easier. They pushed the bar through the hole and twisted it back and forth, up and down, enlarging the hole bit by bit. The trip from Chedalonova to Auschwitz generally took about six hours. Three hours had passed, and the job was not yet finished. Peretz and Mordechai rolled up their sleeves and worked twice as hard.

When the first blow of the iron bar on the wooden wall was heard, all eyes turned to Peretz and Mordechai. Watching them try to widen the hole, some people murmured disapprovingly. As the work progressed, the complaints became louder. Finally, when the job was finished and it was clear that a hole large enough to jump through had been made, strong protests were heard.

"If even one Jew is missing from this car, the Nazis will punish us all. There is no doubt what our end will be. The hole you made will infuriate them and we will all be held responsible!"

Peretz and Mordechai were dismayed at the sharp criticism. Should they try to save their own skins at the possible expense of their fellow Jews? Had they heard these accusations before, they would never have tried to make the hole, but in all the noise, they had not heard the murmuring. And only now were people protesting loudly.

Instinctively, Peretz and Mordechai turned to the *Rav*. The fateful decision would be up to him.

"It is the right of each individual," declared the *Rav*, "to do everything in his power to save his own life, even if the Nazis may punish others for his actions. In any case, your worries are groundless. Anyone sent to Auschwitz has already been sentenced to death, and no one can die more than once."

Kolonymos and Bathsheva were shaken. What should they do with David? Should they ask Peretz and Mordechai to take him? Bathsheva suggested that they ask the *Rav*, but this was difficult. He was all the way on the other side of the car. Everyone had crowded together to make room for him to sit, and now they could not possibly get across the car to him. Kolonymos, not wanting to shout his question out loud for all to hear, turned to his neighbor and asked him to pass the question on until it reached the *Rav*'s ears.

After a few moments, the *Rav* announced, "A young boy

is here in this car. Anyone who can help him escape from the train will be deserving of God's blessing."

Bathsheva and Kolonymos heard the *Rav*'s answer, but David, although he heard the *Rav*'s words, did not understand that they referred to him until Kolonymos asked if he wanted to escape together with Peretz and Mordechai. Frightened, David began to cry. He was afraid to leave without his parents and he was afraid to jump. Bathsheva stroked his head while Kolonymos spoke soothing words. He explained that if Peretz and Mordechai took him, he would not be in any danger. They would see to his safety.

As they spoke, the train began to slow down. It was coming to a turn. Kolonymos turned to Peretz and asked if he would take David. Peretz was glad to try to save Shlomo's younger brother. David, hearing his father speak to Peretz, realized that the decision had already been made for him.

"Mordechai and I will jump first," Peretz said. "When we are out, lift David up to the hole and direct him to jump far forward, in the direction the train is headed, and to roll over a few times when he hits the ground. Boys his age are agile, so don't worry about him. We'll pick him up afterwards and take him with us."

There was no more time to talk, for the train had already slowed down. Peretz stood beside the hole, Mordechai in front of him. Hup! Mordechai jumped. Hup! Peretz, too, was out. Kolonymos, his hands trembling, picked David up and in a voice choked with emotion, he whispered, "Jump!" Bathsheva hid her face in her hands. She couldn't watch. A minute later the train picked up speed and rushed on toward Auschwitz.

No sound of crying was heard in the car. Bathsheva's and Kolonymos' eyes were dry. These poor people had not lost all feelings of mercy; they simply could not cry. They had no more tears left. Their hearts were crying, but their eyes were dry. On the train to Auschwitz no one cries.

✱ 18 ✱ *After the Jump*

David jumped off the train, did a few somersaults on the ground and stood up on his feet. He even managed to catch a glimpse of the train as it disappeared around the bend. He stood there, watching his father and mother going further and further away from him. Even after the train had disappeared completely, David remained rooted to the spot, not remembering why he was there.

It took a few minutes until he finally recalled that Peretz and Mordechai were supposed to get him. He looked around to see if they had come. He waited a few more minutes, but no one was in sight. Then he began to worry. Perhaps they had forgotten about him? David began to run back along the train tracks. They had jumped first and were therefore behind him. After a few hundred yards, David caught sight of Peretz lying quietly on the ground.

"I'm coming, Peretz," he cried.

But Peretz did not answer. As he approached Peretz, David, short of breath from his run, called out once again.

"Peretz, I was afraid you had forgotten me!"

But again, there was no answer. David began to worry. Was Peretz perhaps ignoring him? Had he decided not to take him along? David reached the spot where Peretz was lying. He bent over and grabbed Peretz's hand, ready to beg to be taken along.

"Vey!" he cried. Peretz's hand was limp, and his eyes, though open, were sightless. He was dead.

Recalling that Mordechai had jumped first, David left Peretz and began to run on, looking for Mordechai. He caught sight of him, also lying on the ground. David stopped running and began to walk slowly. What would he do if Mordechai was dead too? As David approached him, he called out "Mordechai!", hoping that Mordechai would respond, but there was no answer.

David stood still. He did not want to find Mordechai dead. If Mordechai was dead, who would take him away from here? Perhaps Mordechai would get up and come over to him. He was standing so close that Mordechai could not help but notice him . . . if he were alive. But Mordechai did not get up. He, too, was dead. David knew this even before he went over to see for sure. Neither Peretz nor Mordechai had jumped well enough.

David was in a state of shock. He stood beside the dead Mordechai, not knowing where to go. He didn't cry. Peretz and Mordechai were both dead, and his parents were on the train, far away. What was the point of crying if there was no one to hear him? As David thought of his father and mother on the train together with all their fellow Jews, he felt jealous. At least they were together. He was all alone. He looked around him, wondering where to go.

Perhaps he would not go anywhere. There was no one he knew anywhere, so what did it matter where he went, or if he went? He would sit down right where he was. At least he was near Mordechai who had been his friend. He could possibly find people who were alive, but he would not know them and they would not be his friends.

David sat there for a long while, until the pains began. It had been hours since he had last eaten or drunk, and his last meal had not been very substantial. Hunger forced him to start walking. "What a pity," he thought. "If not for my hunger, I could have remained with Mordechai."

He had no idea where to go, nor did he care. He walked only because he was too hungry to sit still. It didn't matter where he went. There was no place for him anywhere in the world.

David followed his own feet, on and on, until he stopped, startled by a barking dog. In the direction of the barking, David saw a few straw-thatched rooftops and realized that he had come to a village. One of the peasants came out of his house and saw David. He chased the dog away and went up to the boy, examining him from head to toe.

"Come with me," he said gently.

Although not very fluent in Polish, David could understand the peasant's speech. He knew that all Poles were anti-Semites and liable to harm him, but he was not afraid of this man. His father and mother were far away, and Peretz and Mordechai were both dead. Nothing less than a miracle could save him now. Not expecting help from any human being, he had lost all fear.

Perhaps, too, being alone seemed so terrible, that David was happy to see anyone, even a Pole. A short while ago, he had felt as though no one but he was alive in the entire world. He belonged to no one and no one cared about him. Then this Pole appeared and took him in.

The Pole offered David a chair in the kitchen, where an elderly woman was busy at the stove. She looked at David, but didn't say a word. The peasant whispered something to his wife, who took out a whole loaf of bread and a bowl full of butter and set them on the table before David.

He stared at the food, unable to believe what his eyes were seeing. It was like the miraculous tales he had heard in *cheder* about the prophet Elijah, who appeared to righteous people and saved them from distress. David was sure that the peasant must be the prophet Elijah in disguise, and that the house and woman were none other than miraculous creations sent from Heaven to save him. The starving boy began to eat and drink with great appetite, fully expecting that the prophet Elijah would then bring him to his father and mother.

When he finished his meal, the peasant asked, "Who are you, child?"

David thought, "Elijah must certainly know all about me, but since he has taken on human form, he is behaving like any person of flesh and blood would behave."

When the peasant repeated his question, David told him the story of the train. The peasant nodded his head and said, "You can stay here as long as you like."

"Thank you, but I want to go back to my father and mother," David replied.

The peasant sighed and said, "I am sorry, my boy, but that is not in my power to fulfill."

David was surprised to hear that Elijah couldn't fly him through the sky to his parents in Auschwitz. Too polite to express his surprise out loud, he was silent.

The peasant went on speaking, "Since there are wicked people in this world, and they hate Jews, you must be very careful. Pretend that you are mute, so that people in the village don't try to speak to you and ask who you are and what you are doing here."

David nodded.

"You will help me in the barn and in the field," the peasant continued, "but whenever you are not working, stay in the house and don't go walking around outside."

"All right," answered David.

"It's not as right as you may think," replied the peasant, "but you're better off here than in Auschwitz."

David could not understand that. Why was it better for him to be here, all alone, than in Auschwitz together with his father and mother? But he did not ask.

David was sure that this peasant was Elijah, but in truth he was just a plain, simple peasant. Nevertheless, he *was* different from other peasants, for Jewish blood ran in his veins. His name was Ivan Ivanovich. His father, at the age of eight, had also been called Ivan. But before that, his name had been Ephraim.

As a child Ephraim had fallen victim to Czar Nikolai's decree to conscript young Jewish boys into the Russian army. Ephraim's father had died when he was very young, and his mother did not have enough money to bribe the authorities to exempt her son from service. So at the age of eight, he was conscripted and sent to a colony of Cantonists.

As time passed, he forgot his family and his religious practices, remembering only that he had once been a Jew. After serving in the army for over thirty years, Ivan was released. He married a Russian woman who bore him three sons.

Ivan, the second son, was now over sixty. He had moved to Poland when it was still under Russian domination, before the Bolshevik revolution. After the revolution, Poland regained its independence, and Galicia, once a part of Austria, was annexed to it. Ivan then moved to Galicia, where his mother's relatives had left him a small heritage of land in the village of Agadatke. Ivan's nephews still lived in Russia, in the Ukraine, and one had a mute son David's age. The villagers knew of him. Now that the border between Russian and Poland was open, Ivan's nephew could have sent one of his sons to help the childless old man on his farm. Ivan told his neighbors that David was his nephew's mute son.

As a child, Ivan had heard about the persecution of the Jews from his father. He told him how he had been forcibly conscripted into the army and turned into a Cantonist instead of what he himself had wanted to become. Ivan's father never forgot that he had wanted to remain a Jew, but the Czar had forced him to forget his Judaism. Jewish blood still flowed in Ivan's veins and a Jewish heart still beat in his chest. Therefore he kept David in his house, and David was confident that his salvation was at hand.

✱ 19 ✱ *In the Labor Camp*

Shlomo had found a friend. Rav Yonathan of Rishakova was also in the labor camp in Russia. Ten years older than Shlomo, he had been a child during the Bolshevik revolution. His father, the *Rav* of Rishakova, had continued to teach him Torah even after all the *yeshivoth* and *chadorim* in Russia were closed. Although he was warned that it was against the law to teach Torah to Jewish children, his father had paid no heed to these warnings and had continued to teach his son Yonathan and a few other boys.

One night two militiamen knocked on his door. The Rabbi, who was teaching the boys just then, was perfectly aware who was knocking and who these uninvited guests must be. He signaled to the boys to hurry out the back door, but the militiamen, who were Jewish, knew all the tricks and had already set up an ambush at all the entrances to the house. The boys fell straight into their trap. The militiamen brought them back into the house, lined them up before the *Rav* and said, "Here are the witnesses that you have transgressed the law!"

"That law is invalid," answered the *Rav*.

"What makes you think that?"

"Because it is overruled by the promise we made at Mount Sinai to teach the Torah to the People of Israel," said the *Rav*.

The boys were sent home and the *Rav* was taken away. To this day, Yonathan knew nothing of his father's fate. All his requests for information on his father's whereabouts had been ignored by the N.K.V.D.

From that day on, Yonathan taught himself. When he grew up, the Jewish community of Rishakova elected him to succeed his father as their Rabbi. He followed in his father's footsteps, secretly teaching Torah to a small group of youngsters.

The picture of that night, when his father was arrested, never left him. Instead of deterring him, it strengthened him. Rav Yonathan had inherited his father's dedication to the cause and had no fear of the government. He continued to practice and teach the Torah, successfully evading the N.K.V.D. for some time, until finally he, too, was arrested and sentenced to ten years of hard labor in a work camp.

When Shlomo arrived, Rav Yonathan had already served three years. His mother, his wife and two young children were waiting for him at home.

Shlomo was deeply impressed by Rav Yonathan's courage. Even here in the camp, surrounded by anti-Semitic Gentiles who breathed fire whenever the word "Jew" was mentioned, Rav Yonathan was not intimidated—neither by the government nor by the populace. He even refused to work on Shabbath, claiming that he accomplished in six days what he had been assigned to do in seven.

This was no easy feat, as the work was backbreaking.

More shacks and buildings were being erected nearby, either as an enlargement of the present camp or as an additional settlement. Deep pits had to be dug for the foundations of the new buildings, and they were dug by hand. A man would stand inside a deep, narrow hole whose diameter was only slightly wider than his own body, wielding a short-handled spade. As he dug, he would have to throw the dirt high up out of the pit or else it would fall back down on his head. Every day a large number of workers were punished for not completing their quota, and they received a smaller ration of food than usual. The *Rav*, on the other hand, would do more than his daily quota each day.

What gave him such strength? It was neither hunger nor the desire to receive a full ration of bread. If that were sufficient motivation, everyone would accomplish this feat, as there was no one in the camp who was not constantly hungry. It was not his physical strength either, as some of the peasants in the camp were much stronger than the *Rav*.

What, then, gave him his extra strength? It was the fear that if he did not finish the seven day quota in six days, he would be forced to work on Shabbath.

Nevertheless, Rav Yonathan did not succeed in convincing the camp director and the N.K.V.D. officer. They simply claimed that if he could do more than the accepted daily quota, then his daily quota should be raised, in which case he had not yet completed his quota for the seventh day. Furthermore, they considered his very attempt to observe Shabbath as a crime. Although Soviet law allowed for freedom of religion, this referred to the private, not the public, sector. By publicly abstaining from work on Saturdays, the

Rav might influence other Jews in the camp to observe Shabbath, in which case he would be disseminating religious propaganda.

Rav Yonathan had already been sentenced to solitary confinement several times for this "crime." He was often thrown into a cell less than six feet square, where he could neither spread out comfortably nor walk around. For days at a time he would sit or stand or lie with his legs folded in this cramped space, his whole body bent together, subsisting on a small ration of bread, just enough to keep him from starving.

One might object that even in the labor camps the diet included more than bread. Soup was served every day—a thin watery potato or beet borsht containing a few crumbs of pork fat or meat. Unwilling to eat nonkosher food, the *Rav* subsisted on bread alone. According to Jewish law anyone whose life is in danger may eat forbidden foods. As a rabbi, Yonathan was certainly aware that this law applied to him, for he was getting weaker by the day and would not be able to go on much longer on bread alone. Nevertheless, he chose the hard way. He took upon himself even those restrictions from which he was exempt. He chose to do even more than the Torah required.

Shlomo was deeply impressed by Rav Yonathan's behavior. Nevertheless he made no attempt to imitate him. Only a man who was committed heart and soul could do what Rav Yonathan was doing, and Shlomo was still torn between two worlds. The "two Shlomos" were still at war within him. Since Birobidzhan, Shlomo of the *Beith Midrash* had gained the upper hand, but he had not yet succeeded in completely exorcizing the other Shlomo. This would take a long time.

Shlomo of the *Beith Midrash* was strongly attracted to Rav Yonathan. Every day after work he would seek out the *Rav*'s company. After a few conversations, the *Rav* realized that he was talking to two people.

"I can see from your conversation that you are a *talmid chacham*. What, then, made you do such a stupid thing and immigrate to Soviet Russia?" asked Rav Yonathan.

"From Chedalonova I immigrated to Eretz Yisrael," answered Shlomo, "but when I saw that even in Eretz Yisrael Jews were hemmed into a ghetto, I rebelled. I fled to Russia, believing that here at last, there would be no anti-Semitism."

At his mention of Eretz Yisrael, Shlomo saw a tremor run through Rav Yonathan's body.

"How I envy you! You were in Eretz Yisrael!" he exclaimed. "How I wish I could go! That was the greatest mistake you could have made—to leave Eretz Yisrael! Eretz Yisrael is every Jew's home. No man deserts his own home just because he has trouble with the neighbors. A man who has his own home can stand up to his enemies and defend his honor. People may hate him, but they won't deride him.

"Anti-Semitism respects no borders. It thrives wherever there are Jews, even in Eretz Yisrael. Esau's hatred of Jacob began in Eretz Yisrael, and from there it spread throughout the world. You made one mistake after another. How could you—a Jew—even *imagine* that there might be some place in the world free of anti-Semitism?

"From the day that we stood at Mount Sinai, the rest of

the world has hated us. Even a Jew who runs away from Mount Sinai, denying the religion of Moshe *Rabbeinu* and the Jewish people, cannot succeed in escaping this hatred. The fragrance of Sinai clings to every Jew, whether he is aware of it or not, and this fragrance arouses the hatred of the Gentile world."

Shlomo listened intently and then asked, "You have spoken from your heart, but if what you say is true, then what should we do about it?"

"Do about what?" asked the *Rav*.

"Do about anti-Semitism," replied Shlomo.

"That is not within my control, and therefore it is not a problem for me to solve. I make no attempt to stop the Gentiles from hating me; I simply try to develop within myself the power to withstand that hatred."

"What power is that?" asked Shlomo.

"A man who fully understands why he is suffering finds it much easier to suffer. It is hardest for a man to suffer when he has no idea why, or to what end, he is suffering. The stronger I become as a Jew, the easier it is for me to bear the hatred of the Gentile. Therefore I try to make myself the strongest Jew I can possibly be."

After that, the daily discussions between Shlomo and the *Rav* revolved around one main topic—the meaning of being a Jew.

Noticing the growing friendship between the two, the camp supervisor began to interrogate Shlomo, asking him, "What do you and Yonathan talk about all the time?"

"We have much in common," answered Shlomo.

"What is that?" insisted the supervisor.

"We are both Jewish," answered Shlomo.

"But there is no racial discrimination in the U.S.S.R.," protested the supervisor.

"Oh yes there is," replied Shlomo. "Jews are hated."

"They are not hated because they are Jewish, only because they are traitors to the Russian homeland. Throughout the whole world, Jews are known to be traitors to their homeland."

These were the very same words that Shlomo had heard from the N.K.V.D. agent in Birobidzhan. Now he realized that this was the *Russian* excuse for anti-Semitism, although the anti-Semitism itself was the same in all places. Each country found its own particular reason to voice the same hatred.

Little by little, Rav Yonathan's words made an inroad into Shlomo's heart, until one day he reached a decision: he must try to imitate Rav Yonathan. On Thursday and Friday he finished his quota for three days, and on Saturday Shlomo did not report for work. When the supervisor came by to find out what was wrong, Shlomo answered that he had already done his quota for that day. On that Shabbath both Shlomo and Rav Yonathan were thrown into solitary confinement—Shlomo for not going to work, and Rav Yonathan for disseminating religious propaganda and convincing Shlomo not to work. Shlomo, who was by nature stubborn and independent, declared war on the camp management and refused on principle to work any longer on Shabbath. Being locked up had no more influence on him than it had had on Rav Yonathan.

✱ 20 ✱ *Shlomo Leaves the Camp*

Hitler had violated his pact with Stalin and had invaded Soviet Russia. Stalin, forced to seek aid in repulsing the Nazis, tried to make Soviet Russia look more sympathetic in the eyes of the Western world. The first thing he did was to decrease the number of prisoners in the forced labor camps. Then he invited the Red Cross to visit the camps and see for themselves that these were merely work camps—not places of torture, as the rumors had told. A few crumbs of bread were added to each day's ration, and the work quota was lowered somewhat. Relations between the government and the laborers changed from a master-slave relationship to a worker-employer arrangement. Those prisoners who had never even been formally tried were the first to be released, before the Red Cross investigation committees could ask why they were being held. Next to be released were those prisoners whose "crimes" were not really crimes. Shlomo belonged to the first class of prisoners and Rav Yonathan to the second.

One day, Shlomo was summoned to headquarters by the N.K.V.D. officer. Not informed of the reason for this summons, Shlomo was naturally quite apprehensive. Perhaps it was on account of the trouble he had caused the camp management lately by refusing to work on the Sabbath. Shlomo prepared himself to stand up to the authorities with every ounce of his strength, and to oppose any compromise.

Walking into the building, he was greeted by the officer in charge, but Shlomo failed to recognize him. It was simply not the same man that Shlomo had known before. Never before had this man's face been friendly or worn a smile. Anger had always been stamped on it like a tattoo. Now, some miracle had taken place. There was not a trace of anger left. In its place was a grin! Shlomo stared at the officer in amazement, wondering what could have caused such a transformation.

"It must be a trick," he thought. "The anger that will strike after such a smile will be even more devastating."

The officer shook Shlomo's hand, greeting him as free men outside the camps do. Shlomo returned his greeting, still telling himself, "It must be a trick."

For the first time, the officer gestured to a chair and asked Shlomo to sit down. What was the point of such a show? Shlomo tried to anticipate all the possible tricks such a person might play on him, but he could not solve the riddle, so he sat down and waited.

"We have checked your file and have decided to release you," announced the officer. "This is the strength of Socialist justice. Sooner or later the truth must come out. The minute we discover that a given person is not guilty, we release him. It is unfortunate that circumstances sometimes prevent a man's innocence from being discovered in time, but of course no man may be released until proven innocent."

Shlomo sat and listened without reacting. He had no way of knowing whether the officer was speaking seriously or playing vicious games with him. The officer reached into his drawer, drew out a piece of paper, and handed it to Shlomo. It was an identity certificate like that held by all free Soviet citizens.

"With this certificate you may travel anywhere in Russia except for those places where the certificate is not valid. If you present it at the train station, you will be given a train ticket. All of Russia is open before you,, except for those areas which are closed."

Shlomo was stunned. He arose, mumbled a thank-you and left. Once outside, Shlomo examined the certificate and wondered whether or not to rejoice. On the one hand, there could be no better grounds for rejoicing than this totally unexpected, newly gained freedom. Who can fathom the joy of a slave who has been freed?

On the other hand, Shlomo had no use for his new-found freedom anymore. He had nowhere to go. The members of Elka's group had all been separated, and he had no idea where his friends could be. Furthermore, he no longer felt much in common with them. His soul had returned to the *Beith Midrash*, and his world was now different from theirs. Even if he succeeded in locating them, he would no longer be comfortable in their company. He felt uprooted. There was no place for him to take his new-found freedom. The only person he was now attached to was Rav Yonathan, from whom it would be very hard to part.

Shlomo went to look for the *Rav* and discuss his problem. He looked all over the camp, but couldn't locate him.

Afraid that the *Rav* had once again been thrown into confinement, Shlomo became depressed. He entered his cabin, lay down and pondered his new status.

His sudden freedom had become a heavy, almost unbearable burden. How could he begin life all over again as a free man? Perhaps he should not leave the camp. He could remain here and work as a citizen, not as a prisoner. Many prisoners who had been freed after ten years of hard labor had chosen to remain in the camp. They had nowhere else to go anymore.

On second thought, Shlomo decided that this might be a satisfactory solution for a Gentile, but not for himself. How could any Jew who wanted to retain his identity settle among the Gentiles? The longer he stayed here, the more he felt cut off from other Jews and from Eretz Yisrael.

"How mistaken it is to imagine that good news automatically brings happiness. That is simply not true. I, for example, have just received the best news possible, that I have been freed from slavery, and nevertheless I am suffering. Instead of rejoicing, I am miserable."

Suddenly, Shlomo heard his name whispered. He jumped up and saw Rav Yonathan, looking very sad, at his bedside. The *Rav* stood there, clearing his throat as if he had something very important to say, but didn't know quite how to begin. Just as Shlomo was about to tell the *Rav* his story, the *Rav* himself began to speak, measuring his words carefully, as if afraid to voice them out loud.

"I have just come from the N.K.V.D. headquarters," he announced, pausing to look at Shlomo. Noticing the suffering in his face, he continued apologetically, "I am both happy and sad at this moment. What I was told would ordinarily be considered very good news."

"Did we perhaps both receive the same news?" interrupted Shlomo joyously.

"I was told that I am now a free man," answered Shlomo.

The *Rav*'s face lit up and he sighed with relief. "Then why do you look so sad, Shlomo?" he asked. "There is no happier news than that!"

"You wonder about me? Look at your own face! If you received the same news, why did you look so forlorn?" Shlomo answered.

"I was sad for your sake," said the *Rav*, "but now that I know that you, too, are a free man, all my sadness has vanished. Only happiness remains!"

Shlomo's face fell. "How can I rejoice when I have nowhere to take my new-found freedom? And how can I leave you after I have become so attached to you?"

The *Rav* lifted his forefinger and sang his answer in the tune used to learn *gemara*. "I am surprised at you, Shlomo, for not being able to answer your own questions. In your youth you were a diligent student of the Torah. You should know that it is always easier to answer two questions than one. If there is only one question, one must search for an answer, and it is not always easy to find. But if there are *two* questions, they must answer each other.

"For instance, if you didn't know where to go, but were not attached to me, then you would have to search elsewhere for the answer. Or on the other hand, if you had somewhere to go, but found it too hard to part from your close friend, you would really have a difficult problem to solve. But now, if, as you say, you have nowhere to go and you are attached to me, then the two problems solve each other. You will come with me and that will solve both your problems!"

Tears welled up in Shlomo's eyes.

"There is nothing finer than tears of joy," Rav Yonathan consoled him.

The very next day, Rav Yonathan and Shlomo left the forced labor camp and started out for Rishakova. It took weeks for them to reach their destination. Because of the war, all the roads were out of commission. Trains did not follow any timetable and were so overcrowded that they could take no more passengers. People stood hanging on the stairs or on the tops of cars, holding onto anything imaginable in order to reach their destination. To men who had just gone from slavery to freedom and from darkness to light, such adventures were child's play. Their great joy lightened their difficult trip. Slowly, bit by bit, they came closer and closer to their destination—Rishakova.

When they finally arrived, the *Rav* decided to go to a friend's house first, afraid that if he simply walked into his own home, the shock would be too great for his family to bear. As the members of his friend's family recognized him, exclamations of surprise and joy flew through the air. His friend's wife ran to break the news to Yocheved, Rav Yonathan's wife, and to his son and daughter, and to prepare them for the reunion.

Meanwhile the *Rav* listened to all the news about his fellow Jews since he had left. The Germans had come quite close and had almost conquered their town, but at the last minute, thank God, they were repulsed by the Red Army, and the town was saved.

Through the window, the *Rav* caught sight of his wife and children on their way to the house. Full of excitement he rose and went to the door to meet them. Yocheved and the children came in, the children falling straight into their father's arms. Yocheved stood there, her face radiating happiness as she watched her husband and her children embrace. Two gigantic tears of joy glistened in her eyes.

"Now let me say hello to your mother," said the *Rav* to his children.

He and Yocheved stood there, exchanging looks of happiness mingled with sorrow. The *Rav* had wondered why his mother had not come to greet him, but when he looked into his wife's eyes, he understood that his mother would come no longer. Later, when they were alone, there would be time enough to discuss all of their personal affairs.

"I brought a young friend with me from the camp," he said, turning to Shlomo.

"Welcome," Yocheved smiled.

Shlomo nodded his head in greeting to the *Rebbetzin.*

"Let us go home," said the *Rav*, and the two men, Yocheved and the children left the house together. Within a few hours, the whole town knew that the *Rav* had returned from the camp. The stream of friends eager to welcome him and share his happiness began. For several days the door opened and closed continuously all day long and halfway through the night.

In Rishakova no one was exempt from work, not even the *Rav*. To the Soviet government, teaching Torah or serving as a rabbi was not an honorable profession. An adult must work at a recognized job, so the *Rav* and Shlomo both decided to join the bookbinders' cooperative. All kinds of books were brought to them to mend and bind, including *gemaroth* and other old, worn Jewish books. As the *Rav* and Shlomo sat and bound these books, they would browse through those that interested them, renewing their ties with the Torah's knowledge.

Shlomo did not intend to remain in Rishakova forever, but the *Rav* advised him to wait until the war was over and transportation was not so difficult. Then they would find a way to send him back to the place he came from.

✱ 21 ✱ *Zissel in Despair*

Soon after Mrs. Blitz disappeared, Mrs. Chasidov of Nachrovah visited her sister in Chedalonova. Needless to say, she was extremely upset by the news of Rozeshka's disappearance. She usually brought back a letter for Zissel from Mrs. Blitz each time she went to Chedalonova. Now she would return empty-handed. What could she tell Zissel? Would Zissel decide to risk her own life by going to search for her missing mother? The two sisters-in-law spent hours discussing the matter and finally decided not to tell Zissel that her mother had disappeared.

Chasidova returned home and gave Zissel regards from her mother, but Zissel immediately asked for her letter.

"She didn't write this time. She only sent regards," said Chasidova. "Perhaps she had nothing special to say."

"That's impossible!" exclaimed Zissel, searching Chasidova's face. "My mother would never begrudge her only daughter a few lines on paper, if only to write and assure me that all was well."

"I don't know why she didn't write," Chasidova responded. "All I can tell you is that this time she sent you her regards."

"Then I will go to Chedalonova and see for myself," decided Zissel. "Perhaps all is not well with her."

"Oh, no, that is much too dangerous a trip," objected Chasidova. "Evil people on the streets search the eyes of any stranger and follow his footsteps."

"But I made several visits to the convent and nothing ever happened to me," protested Zissel.

Chasidova realized that she would not be able to prevent Zissel from traveling to Chedalonova unless she disclosed the whole truth.

"Do you really want to know the truth about your mother?" she asked.

"Of course I do!"

"Well, the truth is that I don't know either," answered Chasidova.

Shocked, her voice trembling with fear, Zissel ventured, "Why, how could that be? You have just come back from Chedalonova, from the very house where my mother is supposed to be hiding!"

Chasidova stood up and told Zissel the story of her mother's disappearance, of how she had simply walked out of the house and not returned.

Zissel threw herself down on her bed, weeping until her pillow was drenched with tears. Chasidova let her cry, making no effort to console her. She knew there was nothing she could possibly say to comfort Zissel. She also knew that Zissel must cry herself out. Only her tears could wash the pain from her heart.

For a long time Zissel lay in bed, filled with the calamity that had befallen her. Her mind was ablaze with grief and sorrow, and from this grief and pain came forth a decision: to return to the ghetto. Since she no longer had any relatives alive outside of the ghetto, she would return to Bathsheva, who was now her only mother. No daughter should forsake her mother in times of danger. So long as her own mother had been outside the ghetto and had wanted her nearby, Zissel had acceded to her request, especially since Bathsheva had also told her to follow her mother.

But now that her own mother was no longer alive, Zissel felt that Bathsheva's request no longer applied. Zissel felt that the responsibility of watching over Sarah had only been an excuse that Bathsheva used to convince Zissel to save herself.

Zissel had no hope that her mother was still alive. She was as aware as anyone else of the treatment accorded Jews caught outside the ghetto confines. There could be no more convincing proof that her mother's identity had been discovered, and that she had been handed over to the Germans, than the fact that she had not returned to Chasidova's house.

When her plans to return to the ghetto began to take on more detailed form, Zissel decided to discuss the matter with Chasidova. Seeing that she had calmed down and had stopped crying a bit, Chasidova invited Zissel to eat lunch.

"I'm not hungry," said Zissel. "All I want now is to return to the ghetto in Chedalonova."

"There is no one left there to return to, my daughter," said Chasidova quietly.

"What? What did you say?"

Her voice steeped in sorrow, Chasidova replied, "Many tragedies have befallen us in this world. It is not within our power to reverse them."

"Where are all the Jews who lived in the ghetto of Chedalonova?" cried Zissel.

"The Nazis did not make any public announcements when they took the Jews away, but I heard rumors that they were transported to Auschwitz," was her answer.

Zissel herself had guessed the answer to her own question, even before she had asked, but she could not face the truth until it was explicitly told to her. Zissel did not eat at all that day, nor did she close her eyes that night.

The days following were difficult ones for her. Slowly, bit by bit, she began to realize that Kolonymos and Bathsheva had indeed sent her to watch over Sarah. They knew what the future had in store for them. They had foreseen their fate and had wanted Zissel to live—both for her own sake and so that someone remained alive to watch over their daughter. Gradually, protecting Sarah became the main goal of Zissel's life. It was no incidental duty, it was her sole reason for living. She decided that she must visit Sarah more frequently and pay closer attention to the poor orphan entrusted to her care.

As soon as she had partially recovered from the shock of the bad news, Zissel decided to return to the convent. She had to work very hard to improve her appearance. The two tragedies that had befallen her family and loved ones had left their mark on her. All her grief was reflected in her eyes, and her young face was veiled in sorrow. She could never appear on the street looking like that. She must erase all signs of sadness and act as if she had no cares.

This was not easy. Zissel worked very hard at making herself look young and happy and carefree. Chasidova followed her progress and finally assured her that she looked perfectly fine and could safely leave the house.

Zissel walked to the convent just as she had so many times before, not expecting any surprises. This time, however, was different. The moment she met Maria she knew that something had changed. Zissel greeted Maria as if she were an old friend, but Maria barely returned the greeting. She did not look directly at Zissel, and she answered her while busying herself with something else.

"I have come to visit Sarah," announced Zissel.

"We do not allow strangers to visit the girls," stated Maria.

"I am no stranger," protested Zissel. "Her father and mother have sent me to visit her."

Maria raised her head and said, "You are lying. Sarah's parents did not send you."

"Why should I lie?" asked Zissel.

"If you really come from Chedalonova and know Sarah's family well, then you must certainly know that the Germans have liquidated the ghetto. Sarah's parents could not possibly have sent you here." Maria looked at Zissel with colorless eyes, a victorious note in her voice.

Zissel did not hesitate a moment. "Certainly I know of the tragedy that befell the Sharfson family, but the request to watch over Sarah was not put to me today or yesterday. It was a long time ago. This is certainly not the first time I have come here to visit her."

Maria, a look of open hatred on her face, replied, "Now that Sarah has neither father nor mother, we are her guardians. She was entrusted to our care, and we will watch over her. You need not bother yourself any longer. You can depend on us. The Church knows how to be merciful, so Sarah has no need of anyone else's mercy."

She paused, then added loudly, "Certainly not the mercy of Jews." Two knives shot out of Maria's eyes, straight into Zissel's heart.

As Maria shouted these last words, the door opened and Tzorerkeh and Sinavkeh came out of the adjoining room, followed by the six Jewish girls, including Sarah, who was the eldest. Seeing them, Maria glared angrily at the two nuns and motioned the girls back.

But it was too late. Sarah had already seen Zissel. She ran to her and refused to leave the room. Maria did not want to physically pull Sarah away, so she said, "Very well. This time I will allow you to speak to Sarah. But it is the last time."

Zissel needed all her strength to face Sarah. She asked Sarah how she felt and if all was well, but instead of answering, Sarah asked, "How are my mother and father?"

Zissel evaded the question.

"You are a bright girl, Sarah. You will always be able to take care of yourself."

Suddenly, Zissel bent over and covered Sarah with kisses, sobbing and holding her tightly. Frightened, Sarah also began to cry. Maria immediately came in, took Sarah's hand, and pulled her out of the room. Zissel stood rooted in her place and could only repeat, "Take care of yourself."

Zissel was left standing alone. She left the convent and walked quickly back to Chasidova's house. It was best to get back as fast as possible, before someone on the street could take note of her tear-drenched face.

As soon as Zissel walked through the door, Chasidova understood that something had happened at the convent, but she was wise enough not to question Zissel. Even if she had, Zissel would probably not have been able to answer her, for her heart was overflowing with despair.

✷ 22 ✷ *Shlomo Finds David*

As long as the war continued, there was no way for Shlomo to go back to Poland. Only after the war was over did he find a way to return. As a Soviet citizen, it was illegal to leave Soviet Russia without an official exit permit, and that of course was impossible to obtain. Luckily, Shlomo found a way to smuggle himself across the border.

As a result of the war, there were many Polish refugees in Russia—people who had fled from Nazi Poland to Russian Poland—and these Poles had been classed as aliens and exiled to Siberia. Now that the war was over and Poland had become a Soviet satellite, these refugees were being shipped back to Poland in special freight trains. These trains stopped to refuel near Rishakova and at other stations, and the passengers had a chance to buy food. At each stop, a few Jews would manage to sneak onto the train and cross the border back into Poland. On their way into Siberia the trains had been heavily guarded, for then the passengers were classified as enemy aliens. But now the guard on duty was lax and it was fairly easy to sneak on without being detected. Shlomo was one of many who crossed the border from Russia to Poland this way.

The first place Shlomo headed for was Chedalonova. He combed the town thoroughly, but was unable to locate a single Jewish soul until he reached the cemetery. There he found many Jews—all those who had died before he left for Eretz Yisrael and many who had died afterwards. Unfortunately, Shlomo could not identify any of the graves as the stones had been uprooted and were scattered all over. Nevertheless, he knew that the dead had not been uprooted; these were the Jews of Chedalonova.

Shlomo continued on to Temyonovah and Nachrovah. He found Jews everywhere, but not live ones.

Shlomo wandered from one cemetery to the next until he finally reached Cracow. There he found several hundred Jews who were still among the living. None were originally from Cracow; most came from small towns where only one or two Jews had survived. After the war they had drifted to Cracow, that renowned center of Jewish learning, to join their few surviving brothers.

These Jews had no place in Cracow, just as they had no place in the rest of Poland. All of Poland was one huge Jewish cemetery—not a fit place for any Jew to live. The refugees in Cracow were temporarily housed in government buildings while they waited to find a permanent place for themselves somewhere else in the world. Meanwhile, their primary concern was to locate their relatives and friends, those who might have survived the tidal wave of fire and blood that had wiped out the entire Jewish world of Poland.

Upon arrival, each refugee registered at the American Joint Rescue Committee office, and received food and clothing donated by American Jewry. Copies of these registration lists were posted daily on the walls of the Joint offices, and all those who had arrived in Cracow could search the lists for familiar names. Each new arrival would write his own name and then read through the names of all those who had registered previously.

Every day, the veterans would check the lists anew, searching for familiar names among the newcomers. Besides this continuous search for names and faces, there was nothing else for the Jewish refugees to do in Cracow.

Shlomo, too, signed up at the Vaad offices for his food and clothing, and read the lists of names like everyone else. The lists were in alphabetical order, and Shlomo always went straight to the letter *shin*. One day he let out a gasp. There on the list was "Sharfson, David of Chedalonova"! There could be no mistake. Only one David Sharfson had lived in Chedalonova.

Shlomo ran to the clerk and asked where he could find David. The clerk consulted his records and told him that David Sharfson was in the Youth Aliyah dormitory with the other young boys. They would soon be on their way to Eretz Yisrael. Receiving directions from the clerk, Shlomo ran breathlessly to look for David.

Several years had passed since they had parted, but the two brothers recognized each other immediately. Shlomo recognized David because he knew that David was in the dormitory, and David recognized Shlomo because Shlomo still looked the same. He had a beard now, but it was not yet full enough to hide his face.

One might have expected such a reunion to be a joyous event. One might have expected two brothers to cry and laugh and hug and kiss each other. But it was not so. As soon as Shlomo recognized David, he went over to him, put his arms around the thin lad and whispered, "David, do you recognize me?"

David looked up at him, and gasped, "Oh, Shlomo!"

Before he could say another word, Shlomo asked in a trembling voice, "Where are Mother and Father?"

David lowered his head and did not answer. Now Shlomo knew what he had already felt before, but then he had only guessed it in his heart; now he read it on David's face. Shlomo took David over to a corner of the room, sat down facing him and asked David to tell him all the things he did not yet know.

David recounted the entire story, beginning with their life in the ghetto together with Rozeshka Blitz and her daughter Zissel. He told Shlomo how Zissel had saved Sarah's life during the first child hunt in the ghetto, and how Mrs. Blitz had left shortly after, leaving Zissel behind. He described how Sarah had been smuggled out to a convent, how Zissel had left the ghetto, and how her mother had returned and been killed by the Nazis when he and his parents were rounded up for Auschwitz. David explained how he had jumped from the train, and how he had found Peretz and Mordechai dead on the tracks. And he told of Ivan Ivanovich, who sheltered and protected him for the duration of the war, and finally brought him to the Joint Committee in Cracow just a few days ago.

As Shlomo listened to David's saga, his soul was in a state of deep turmoil. There was so much to hear and understand and digest all at once. Now he knew that Sarah had been placed in a convent, but he did not know *which* convent. Nor did he know if she had remained there throughout the war, or whether she was still alive. He must also find Zissel, if *she* was still alive. Many Jews had been caught outside the ghetto and had met the same fate as their brethren inside. In the one day he had spent in Cracow he had already managed to hear stories of Jews with forged documents who managed to impersonate Poles. Many had survived, but many others had been caught and killed, either by the Germans or by the Poles themselves. He must search for Zissel, but where?

Shlomo decided that first he would try the Joint Committee lists in Cracow. He had already read the lists through several times and not seen her name. Nevertheless, she might arrive tomorrow or the next day. Cracow was the center for Jewish survivors and newcomers arrived daily. He would stay in Cracow for a while and wait for her. If she did not come, he would search for her in the other towns that served as refugee centers.

Shlomo was anxious to find Zissel for two reasons: to find out about Sarah, and to find Zissel herself. Here in Cracow Shlomo felt much more attached to Zissel than he had felt in Eretz Yisrael. The fact that she had lived in the ghetto with his parents and had shared their sad fate almost to the end, endeared her to him now more than ever before. And he remembered that she had followed him to Eretz Yisrael, even though she herself was no great Zionist. He remembered, too, the unspoken promise he had made to her. Now all these memories and feelings merged, compelling Shlomo to find her.

Shlomo was also busy with David. During the years that David had lived with Ivan he had not looked at a Hebrew letter. Now Shlomo must try to help David make up what he had missed during all those years. Shlomo found an empty room where he could teach Torah to David and his friend, Chaim Glick of Nachrovah. Chaim was a few years younger than David, but there was no difference in the scholastic background of the two. Neither had learned very much. Furthermore, Chaim was very bright, and his sharp mind belied his age. David and Chaim sat and learned for hours each day, absorbing all that Shlomo could teach them.

In his free time, Shlomo checked the lists of new arrivals at the Joint offices, searching for the name "Zissel Blitz of Chedalonova." So far it had not appeared.

* 23 * *Wedding in Cracow*

One day Chasidova burst into the house. She ran straight over to Zissel, wrapped her arms around her and exclaimed happily, "Zushka, my dear, you are saved!"

"What do you mean—I am saved?"

"In town I have just heard that all the Germans have left Nachrovah. They are fleeing for their lives, back to Germany, and the Russians are pursuing them."

Zissel sighed and answered, "Yes, that is very good news, but it has come too late. There is no way to revive the dead."

"Good news, no matter how late it is, is still good news," said Chasidova firmly. "The dead will not come back to life, but at least those who are still living will no longer die."

"That is true. Nevertheless, there is no room for joy in my heart right now." She thought for a moment and then added, "Now that there are no more Nazis in Nachrovah, I have an important mission to carry out."

"What is that?"

"If there are no more Nazis, I need not worry about the nuns informing on me. Now, at last, the time has come to fulfill my mission with Sarah."

Chasidova looked down at the floor, too embarrassed to look Zissel in the eyes. "I doubt that you will be successful. There are rumors that the six Jewish girls from the ghetto are to be baptized in the convent tomorrow."

Zissel jumped up as though bitten by a snake. "No! I will not let them take Sarah away from me. I must go to the convent at once. I will demand that they return Sarah to me. Sarah is Jewish, and her parents sent me here to ensure that she remain Jewish."

"Although I am a Christian, I am ashamed of this forced conversion of the ghetto girls," said Chasidova. "Nevertheless, as a devout Christian, I cannot bring myself to protest against the Church for taking these girls under her wing. You, my daughter, go and try your luck; perhaps you will succeed. It is no longer dangerous for you to be identified as a Jewess."

Without undue preparation, Zissel picked herself up and went to the convent. As she approached the entrance, she saw Tzorerkeh standing at the gate watching her. Tzorerkeh waited until the uninvited guest had approached the gate and was about to enter, and then she blocked the way.

"I have come to see Sarah Sharfson," said Zissel.

"Didn't Maria already warn you not to come here again?" threatened Tzorerkeh.

"I have not come to visit today. I have come to take Sarah away."

Tzorerkeh looked at Zissel with surprise and asked, "Who authorized you to take one of the children out of the convent?"

"The child's parents," answered Zissel.

Tzorerkeh smirked. "In that case, let the parents come in person to get their daughter."

Stung by this cruel joke, Zissel replied, "The blood of those murdered cries out from the earth, and you mock them!"

Tzorerkeh slammed the door in Zissel's face and locked it from the inside, leaving Zissel standing alone on the street. "Well, there is no point in standing beside a locked gate," she thought. "They will never open it as long as I am standing here." She picked herself up and went back home.

She told Chasidova of her conversation with the nun whose name she did not know. Chasidova sighed, but said nothing.

"I must find out what time they plan to baptize the girls tomorrow," said Zissel. "Then I can go in together with all the guests. Perhaps I'll be able to catch Sarah's attention."

Chasidova sighed again and said, "I wish you success, but I am not very optimistic. The time is written on the announcement. Tomorrow morning at ten, the girls are to be baptized. The public is invited to attend the ceremony."

Zissel realized that it would be no simple feat to get Sarah back. She would be all alone among hundreds of Catholics, but she felt she must make the attempt. All the responsibility for Sarah now rested on her shoulders. She owed her own life to Kolonymos and Bathsheva for having sent her out of the ghetto. Now she must try with all her might to save their daughter.

The next morning, Zissel did everything she could to strengthen herself, and by half-past nine she was on her way to the convent. From afar she could already see a large number of men and women entering the convent. When Zissel reached the gate, a husky young Pole blocked her way.

"You stay outside!" he ordered.

"Why?" asked Zissel.

"You are a Jewess," he answered.

At first, Zissel was shocked that he knew she was Jewish, until she saw Tzorerkeh behind him.

"Sarah is my sister," she said. "I will not allow you to rob me of my sister!"

The Pole lifted up his hand and made a fist, threatening to strike Zissel if she didn't back away. A crowd was gathering and listening to the dialogue as they waited in line to enter the convent. Zissel had hoped that some of them would come to her defense and demand that she be allowed in, but she was disappointed. All eyes were turned upon her with open hatred. Just then someone grabbed her arm and pulled her away from the gate. Zissel looked behind her and saw that it was Chasidova. "Let's go!" she whispered. "You are in great danger here!" She pulled Zissel away, leaving the crowd and the convent behind.

"I was wrong," Chasidova said. "I thought that once the Germans left Nachrovah, Jews would be safe here again. Now, after listening to all the evil comments I heard outside the convent, I realize that much time must pass before the shedding of Jewish blood again becomes a crime. Meanwhile you must be careful. You are still in danger."

Zissel was also in despair. She had just been deprived of her reason for living. Would she ever be able to fulfill her mission?

That night Zissel couldn't fall asleep. She lay in bed for

hours, her eyes wide open. Over and over, she reviewed Sarah's plight, unable to think of any scheme for rescuing her from the Church.

Toward morning Zissel fell asleep. Suddenly, she saw Kolonymos standing before her, looking straight into her eyes, his face white as a ghost. He didn't say a word, but Zissel read the blame in his eyes—why had she, Zissel, allowed Sarah to be baptized? Zissel wanted to defend herself—to explain how hard she had tried and why she had failed, but suddenly she saw Bathsheva standing beside her husband. Looking at Bathsheva, Zissel saw the tears in her eyes. She was filled with sorrow for Bathsheva. She wanted to sit beside her and tell her the whole story, but Bathsheva said, "It is unnecessary to tell me. Go and tell Shlomo and David."

Zissel was shocked to hear Bathsheva mention David, who had remained behind in the ghetto with his parents. How could she tell David? She wanted to ask Bathsheva where David was, but she couldn't utter a word. She tried over and over again to voice the question, but could not. Instead, she burst into tears.

Chasidova got up and went into Zissel's room. Zissel was crying in her sleep. Chasidova gently put one hand on her shoulder and said, "It's only a dream, my child."

Zissel awoke immediately. She knew that dreams reflect one's daytime preoccupations; nevertheless she wanted to believe that her dream had a deeper significance. The fact that she had dreamed about David pointed in this direction. She might have subconsciously been thinking about Shlomo, but not about David. She would follow the command given her in her dream—to find Shlomo and tell him that Sarah was in a convent. Now that Zissel had this new goal to fulfill, she had not yet failed in her mission.

Chasidova had mentioned that there were still Jews alive in Cracow. Her neighbors in Nachrovah had told her about them. They were very surprised that after all the Germans had done to the Jews, and after all the help the Poles had given the Germans, there were *still* Jews in Poland! They would never have guessed that such a thing could happen.

"I must reach Cracow. There I will be able to find out how to go back to Eretz Yisrael, to Shlomo. I must find him and fulfill his mother's command to inform him about Sarah."

That very day, Zissel took her leave from the Chasidov family. It was hard for them to part. Both Zissel and Mrs. Chasidov were crying, and even Mr. Chasidov's eyes were moist. Zissel thanked them for everything they had done. It was only because of people like them that she could still go on living. They urged Zissel not to despair; better days would yet come.

The Chasidovs accompanied her to the train station and stayed with her until the train departed. Zissel stood inside, looking out the window, and the Chasidovs stood outside, looking back at her in silence. Whatever there was to say had already been said. As the train departed, Zissel waved good-bye, and the Chasidovs crossed themselves as good Christians do, saying something—probably good wishes—which Zissel did not hear.

Six hours later, Zissel arrived in Cracow. She knew the city well and had no need to inquire after the Jewish survivors. It was obvious that they would be in the Jewish Quarter—in that section which had not been completely destroyed during the war.

Zissel found the offices of the Joint Rescue Committee and after registering, she walked over to the lists on the wall and began to look for familiar names.

When she reached *shin*, she was shocked. "It can't be," she thought. "It must be a mistake. Maybe there is another Shlomo Sharfson. The Shlomo Sharfson I know is in Eretz Yisrael. But the city is listed, too—Chedalonova. There was only one Shlomo Sharfson in Chedalonova."

Examining the list a second time, Zissel found David's name. For some reason she had noticed only Shlomo's name the first time. Now she was even more puzzled. Hadn't David remained in the ghetto with his parents and been transported to Auschwitz? How had he been saved? His hometown was also listed as Chedalonova. The same city could not possibly have been mistakenly listed twice.

Zissel started walking all through the building, searching fruitlessly for David and Shlomo, but finding neither. Exhausted, she finally turned her thoughts to the two slips of paper the clerk had given her. One was her new address, and the other was a coupon for food rations. Zissel decided to go to her new lodgings and to rest for a while.

Walking to the address listed on her slip of paper, she found a small room, with a bed, a pillow and two green sheets. Opposite the bed stood a small table and a shaky uncomfortable chair. Zissel lay down. She was not hungry or in any hurry to receive her daily rations. Gradually, she fell asleep.

After Shlomo had finished his daily lesson with David and Chaim, he went to the office to scan the names of the new arrivals. In a few seconds he reached the letter *beith* and was astounded to see "Blitz, Zissel of Chedalonova." Shlomo was sharper than Zissel. Instead of searching haphazardly, he ran immediately to the clerk to get her address. Before going there, Shlomo walked quickly through all the public rooms and courtyards, thinking that she might be in one of them. When he didn't find her, he went to Zissel's room.

Shlomo knocked on the door several times until a sleepy voice answered, "Yes?" He waited for someone to open the door. Inside, Zissel lay in bed thinking, "I must have dreamt that someone is knocking. I must get up and go back to the office to look for Shlomo."

Shlomo knocked again. This time Zissel jumped up and opened the door. Shlomo and Zissel stood facing each other in the doorway, both of them speechless. At first neither could believe his eyes, but after a few moments Shlomo recovered enough to smile and say, "Don't you know me? I'm Shlomo!"

Beaming, Zissel smiled back. "And I am Zissel!" They both laughed.

Shlomo came into the room. "There is much to tell each other," he said, "stories that cannot be told while standing on one foot. We need hours, perhaps even days. I imagine you haven't eaten yet. Let's walk to the office so you can get your food and eat, and then we'll talk."

Zissel's face became serious. "First of all," she said, "before I tell you the whole story, I must tell you one important thing that cannot be postponed."

"What is that?" asked Shlomo.

"Your sister Sarah is still alive," said Zissel.

Shlomo's eyes opened wide with excitement. "Where is she?"

"Sarah is in the convent of Nachrovah," she answered softly.

Shlomo turned white and his face trembled, but a moment later he regained his composure and said, "As long as she is alive there is still hope."

Zissel was relieved. She had fulfilled Bathsheva's command, and now she would no longer be the only one concerned over Sarah's fate. Shlomo would share her mission. Could there be any better partner than Sarah's own brother?

"Where is David?" she asked.

"He is here in the dormitory. He will be leaving for Eretz Yisrael."

"I want to see him. We were together in the ghetto."

"I know. David has already told me part of your story, and you will tell me the rest yourself. You'll meet him soon. We'll pick him up on the way to the office."

Shlomo and Zissel left her room, locked the door, and went to the office. On their way, they stopped at the Youth Aliyah dormitory for David. David stared at Zissel, surprised and delighted to see her.

"You were probably very angry at me, David, when I left you behind in the ghetto," joked Zissel. "Now I have come to apologize."

"After you left, your mother came back," said David.

Now it was Zissel's turn to be surprised. Her heart

pounding, she asked, "And what happened to her?"

David hesitated and then looked down. "The Nazis shot her just before they put us on the train to Auschwitz," he said softly.

Looking up towards heaven, Zissel said, "Thank God!" and sighed with relief.

"You are thankful?" asked Shlomo.

"My mother left the ghetto because she thought that she could save her own life by becoming a Pole. She didn't want to share the fate of the ghetto Jews. It hurt me terribly to see this. Now I am happy to hear that she came back to the ghetto. She returned to her people and died as a Jewess."

Unwilling to cause Zissel more sorrow, David did not disclose the truth—that her mother had been forcefully returned to the ghetto; she had not returned voluntarily.

"Why should you be so bitter about your mother's desire to leave the ghetto and save her life?" asked Shlomo. "You yourself left the ghetto."

"That is part of the long story which I will tell you later," answered Zissel.

It was almost dark now, time for the evening prayers. A *minyan* of Jews assembled in one room of the Joint offices, Shlomo and David among them. It was only now that Zissel noticed Shlomo's *yarmulka*, although he had been wearing it the entire time. After the prayers, Shlomo returned to Zissel and said, "It's too late to walk through town now. The day is over. Tomorrow morning we'll meet here. While we're walking we'll tell each other the story of our wanderings since we last parted in Eretz Yisrael. Our stories may be long ones."

Shlomo accompanied Zissel to her room and then returned alone to his own. He needed no help in preparing his supper. None of the Joint's meals needed any preparation as they all came from cans: meat, fish, and vegetables. Food that could be eaten cold was eaten straight from the can. Food that had to be heated was placed on a metal plate over a kerosene burner that the Joint had supplied to each person.

Shlomo was the first to arrive at their meeting place the next morning. When Zissel came in, she looked rested and in good spirits. Yesterday she had been relieved of a heavy burden. Now she no longer bore sole responsibility for Sarah. Shlomo wished Zissel a good morning and asked how she had slept. "You already told me once that it is hard to sleep in a new place," Zissel answered.

Shlomo laughed and answered, "Then you told me that you had slept very well."

Zissel laughed. "You have a good memory."

"Now let's start our walk so we can begin our stories. It may take a lifetime to tell them all!"

Shlomo and Zissel began to walk through the Jewish Quarter of Cracow. Most of the buildings were in ruins. None of the synagogues or *Batei Midrash* that Zissel had seen on their first walk were still standing. Shlomo and Zissel walked through the ruins, telling of Birobidzhan, the forced labor camp, and of Rishakova; of the ghetto, outside the ghetto and the convent of Nachrovah; of David on the train to Auschwitz, and of Ivan Ivanovich.

As Shlomo and Zissel approached the famous Rema Synagogue, Shlomo could not believe his eyes. The synagogue had not been destroyed! It stood as if on an island, untouched by the war. What had prevented the Nazis from devastating this synagogue?

Shlomo stopped in front of it. "Do you remember this synagogue?" he asked Zissel.

"Certainly," she answered. "You went in to pray here on our first walk."

Shlomo stood there, still looking at the building. Finally he said, "This is where I would like to have the wedding."

"Whose wedding?" asked Zissel, her heart pounding.

"Ours," answered Shlomo.

Zissel blushed. "Don't you want to return to Eretz Yisrael?"

"Of course. How could one imagine staying here? There is no place in the world for a Jew except Eretz Yisrael."

"Then why should we have the wedding here? Wouldn't a wedding in Jerusalem be more beautiful?"

"This will be our revenge on the Poles and the Nazis. They wanted to wipe us off the face of the earth. Having the wedding here, so they hear the sound of our rejoicing, will be the sweetest revenge possible." He paused, then continued, "Here I've been talking about a wedding without even asking the bride for her consent."

Zissel laughed and said, "I already gave my answer a long time ago."

"Yes," said Shlomo. "But then you were speaking to a different Shlomo who no longer exists. Now there is only the Shlomo of the *Beith Midrash*."

"I once told you that even if you made me a *rebbetzin*, it wouldn't scare me away."

Two days later, Shlomo and Zissel accompanied David

to the train station as he and his friends from Youth Aliyah began their journey to Eretz Yisrael. Shlomo and Zissel would join him later on. Many refugees accompanied the group from Youth Aliyah; some went all the way to Eretz Yisrael, others only as far as the train station. Even those people who themselves planned to immigrate to America accompanied this group in order to ease their consciences, as if to say, "You see, even though we personally don't plan to live there, we, too, love Eretz Yisrael."

A month later, a *chuppah* was set up in front of the Rema synagogue in Cracow and the sound of wedding songs was heard. The groom, Shlomo, walked to the *chuppah* and stood there waiting for his bride, Zissel. Shlomo's face was wet with tears. The veil covering Zissel's face hid her tears. She, too, was crying.

The people who brought the bride and groom to the *chuppah* were strangers, not relatives or friends. It was not a very large wedding—a few dozen people, including two or three rabbis. One performed the wedding ceremony and two others recited the blessings.

After the cup was broken and cries of "*Mazal tov*!" were heard, two Poles passed by, looked at the wedding canopy and heard the rejoicing. They stopped to watch and one commented, "Not even the devil is a match for those damn Jews!"

"If Auschwitz couldn't do them in, there's not a chance in the world we'll ever get rid of them," said the other.

They spit on the ground and swore. "The nerve of those damn Jews!" Finally, they left. Shlomo had had his revenge.

A short time later, Shlomo and Zissel immigrated to

Eretz Yisrael. There was no point in their attempting to search for Sarah in Poland. Anti-Semitism was so rampant that they would have endangered their lives by trying to find a Jewish girl in a convent. But upon their arrival in Israel, the first thing Shlomo did was visit the Chief Rabbi in Jerusalem and tell of his sister in the convent of Nachrovah. He asked the Rabbi to contact the Polish Church and demand that Sarah be returned to her family. The Chief Rabbi traveled to Poland and made every effort to help both Sarah and her friends, but to no avail. The doors and lips of the Church were tightly sealed.

✷ 24 ✷ *David and Brachah*

The years went by. Shlomo and Zissel lived in Jerusalem, where Shlomo was one of the rabbis at Yeshivath ha-Mathmidim. They had two children—Rachel, named after Zissel's mother, and Kolonymos, named after Shlomo's father.

David and his friend Chaim Glick both learned at the same *yeshivah*. They were serious students who were rarely distracted from their studies. There was only one thing that occupied their attention besides their studies, and that was the worry over their lost sisters. Sarah had been entrusted to Chasidova's care in Chedalonova and Brachah, Chaim's sister, had been given into the care of Marussa, a Polish woman from Nachrovah. Neither girl had returned after the war. David and Chaim often spoke of freeing their sisters from the clutches of the Church, but so far they had not found any practical course of action.

David's position was a bit easier than Chaim's, for he did not bear the sole responsibility for his sister's welfare. Shlomo and Zissel shared his worry. In addition, Zissel had personally assumed responsibility for Sarah. Chaim, on the other hand, bore all the responsibility for saving Brachah by himself, for he had no other brothers or sisters, and both his parents had been killed in the holocaust.

One day Chaim appeared in the *yeshivah*, overflowing with excitement, and rushed over to David.

"I have some very important news for both of us!" he blurted out.

David, surprised, looked up from his *gemara* and waited.

"I found my sister Brachah!"

David's eyes widened as he listened to Chaim's amazing story. Chaim had discovered his sister, purely by accident, in a convent right here in Jerusalem!

"And," Chaim continued, "the Polish woman Marussa had put her in the convent in Nachrovah! When I told her that I have a friend whose sister Sarah had also been in the convent in Nachrovah, Brachah said that Sarah had been her best friend! I asked her where Sarah is now, but she doesn't know. She hasn't seen her in years.

"When the war was over, the Jewish girls were all baptized, and their names were changed. Brachah became Barbara and Sarah was called Silvana. They finished elementary school and the theological seminary and were then separated. Each was sent to a different school to work as a missionary teacher." Chaim had finished his story.

"This is not good news for me," David said disappointedly. "I don't know any more now about Sarah's whereabouts than I knew before."

"Nevertheless," rejoined Chaim, "it's easier to search for Silvana in the Catholic missionary school system than it is to look all over the world for Sarah! At least you know where to start."

Realizing that Chaim's words made sense, David said, "Let's tell my brother Shlomo."

"Maybe your sister-in-law Zissel remembers my sister Brachah from her visits to the convent," said Chaim. "Brachah doesn't remember Zissel. I asked her."

Just then Shlomo, now Rabbi Sharfson, came into the room. All the pupils rose in respect for their teacher, returning to their seats only after he was seated. He began the daily lesson, but David's and Chaim's attention wandered far away that morning. They were not to blame if all their thoughts revolved around the story of Brachah's return; nothing else concerned them that day. They sat in class, counting the minutes until the lesson would be over.

After class David walked home with Shlomo, telling him Chaim's story on the way. Shlomo said excitedly, "We must invite Brachah to our house and hear her story in person. I have a feeling that she can help us find Sarah."

As soon as he walked into the house, Shlomo told his wife Zissel about Brachah. Zissel's eyes lit up and she, too, said, "We must invite Brachah here."

David walked over to the rented room where Chaim lived. A girl was sitting inside. David called Chaim out to the corridor and delivered Zissel's invitation to Brachah.

"We will come this evening," said Chaim.

David returned home to tell Zissel that Brachah and Chaim were coming, and Zissel promptly started preparing for the guests.

That evening, Chaim appeared at the Sharfsons' house, accompanied by a lovely young woman with large, dark Jewish eyes. Rav Shlomo greeted Chaim and asked him to be seated. Zissel shook Brachah's hand, trying to remember if she had ever seen her before. Brachah had been one of the six girls who were in the corridor of the convent the last time Zissel had visited there. But many years had passed since then, and she had changed.

Brachah, however, showed visible surprise as she met Zissel. "Sarah told me you were a Pole and your name was Zushka!" she exclaimed.

Zissel laughed and said, "Sarah certainly knew how to keep a secret. I always told her she was a bright girl!"

Zissel invited Brachah to sit down and tell them her story. As she talked, her audience kept looking back and forth, from Brachah to Chaim and from Chaim to Brachah. They were twins, and even now, they looked as alike as two drops of water. Brachah noticed their smiles.

"The resemblance between us is what saved me. Over a year ago, I was sent by the Catholic Mission to Eretz Yisrael to serve as a missionary teacher. I taught in the Convent of St. Paul on 6 Inquisition Street in Jerusalem. Two days ago there was a demonstration of *yeshivah* students against the mission in the courtyard of the school, and my brother Chaim was there. When he saw me, he recognized me at once because I look just like him! He called me, but when I saw him, I fainted. Then the police came and removed the demonstrators, including Chaim.

"The next day, Chaim returned, hoping to catch a glimpse of me again. I kept going out into the courtyard, for I had a feeling he would come back. When we finally saw each other, I picked up and followed him home, without even a good-bye to my friends in the convent. No one there has any idea what has happened to me."

Brachah smiled again and added, "Had Chaim and I not looked so alike, we would never have recognized each other."

Brachah finished her story. Cautiously, Shlomo asked, "Why didn't you return to your people before the meeting with your brother Chaim? You must certainly have remembered that you were Jewish."

"No one raised in a convent and taught Christian doctrines can free himself of his own power. He needs help. When I came to Jerusalem and saw Jews walking down the street who looked just like my father, my Christian faith was shaken. And when a second crisis came along, in the form of a sudden encounter with my only brother, the only surviving member of my family, it was much easier for me to break my bonds with the Church and return to my people."

Brachah paused, then added, "I was sent to Eretz Yisrael because I was such a devout Christian that no one doubted the strength of my convictions. Sarah was not sent to Eretz Yisrael, apparently because she was less firm in her beliefs. It will be easier to rescue her from the mission's net, if only someone from the outside can get to her."

Not only did Brachah look just like Chaim; she was as talented as he and she made a deep impression on Shlomo and Zissel. When Zissel served her company coffee and cake, she noted that Brachah made a blessing before tasting anything.

The guests stayed for a while longer and then went home. When they had left, Zissel asked Shlomo, "What do you think of Brachah as a wife for David?"

Shlomo thought for a while and answered, "She makes a very good impression. I think she might make a fitting partner for David."

Zissel did not let the matter rest. She visited Brachah several times and invited her to their house frequently. David and Brachah were able to spend time together and to discuss many things. Finally, when the time was ripe, Zissel herself spoke to Brachah and to Chaim. Chaim was pleased. It would be a great honor for him to be related to the *Rav*. Brachah, however, objected modestly, "Perhaps I am not yet worthy of your faith in me. After all, I was completely cut off from the Jewish people for many years."

"We have all returned to our Jewish heritage," answered Zissel. "You are no exception."

Brachah thought that Zissel was referring to herself, since she had also spent several years in a Polish home. She didn't know that Zissel was also referring to her husband.

Not long after, an engagement celebration for David and Brachah was held in the Sharfson house. The *tenaim* were read; the traditional plate was broken, and everyone wished the young couple a heartfelt *mazal tov*.

✳ 25 ✳ *Sarah's Return*

After her engagement, as Brachah became a regular visitor to the Sharfson household, she became increasingly aware that Sarah's shadow was still haunting the family, robbing them all of their peace of mind. No matter what topic of conversation they began with, Sarah's name would inevitably be mentioned. Concern over her fate hung like a heavy stone on their hearts. No one could devise any concrete plan for finding Sarah and bringing her back, but they believed firmly that one day, she would eventually return.

Slowly, Brachah came to the conclusion that it was up to her to act. She herself would travel to Poland in search of Sarah. There was no one more fitting for this mission than she, as she had been Sarah's best friend and would be trusted. Also, she spoke Polish fluently and was perfectly at home in the missionary school system.

When Brachah told David of her decision, he was stunned. On one hand, there was nothing in the world he desired more than for Brachah to rescue his sister Sarah. On the other hand, he was concerned for Brachah herself. Would she be in any danger? Or would she be influenced in any way by her renewed contact with the church?

David talked it over with Shlomo and Zissel. After weighing the matter from all sides, Shlomo decided that they should give Brachah a chance. By now he knew Brachah well enough not to worry about her. With her strong character, energy and imagination, there was no need for any concern. Zissel agreed. They convinced David, and Brachah began to prepare for her trip.

She asked David for pictures of his parents. "My brother Shlomo has the only family photograph," he said. "My parents, Sarah and I are in it. It's the picture he took with him when he first went to Eretz Yisrael, and he still has it."

Brachah was pleased with the snapshot. She asked Zissel for her picture, too.

"I didn't save any of my old photographs," said Zissel.

Brachah laughed and said, "Well then, if you have no pictures of yesterday, let me have a picture of today!"

Zissel lost no time and had her picture taken at once.

Brachah packed all that she might need for the long trip in a small suitcase, including her nun's garb, her Polish passport, and the two pictures. She was ready to set sail for Poland. David, Shlomo and Zissel saw her off, their hearts and eyes directed to Heaven with a silent, fervent prayer for her success.

Two weeks later Brachah arrived in Poland. She traveled from one convent to the next, from one missionary center to another, searching fruitlessly for someone who knew of Silvana Borovsky's whereabouts. Brachah began to fear that her trip would be in vain. Nevertheless, she continued her search.

Finally, in the town of Tzlavka, she hit upon good luck.

There she was told that Silvana had indeed been one of their teachers, but had moved to France over a year ago. When Brachah asked why, she was told that there was no longer any work for missionaries in Poland. As long as there were still Jewish survivors of the holocaust or Jewish refugees from Soviet Russia in Poland, it had been a fruitful field for missionary activity. These poor, uprooted, homeless, jobless Jews were easy prey for the mission. For a loaf of bread and a few pieces of clothing, they were prepared to accept the Church's patronage.

But most of the Jewish refugees had all left Poland—some for Israel and others for America or other parts of the free world. Only Jewish Communists were left in Poland, and these had no interest in any religion. In France, however, there was still a sizable Jewish population, mainly Polish Jews in transit and French survivors of the holocaust. There was still work for the mission among these people.

"Perhaps you know Silvana Borovsky's address in France?" asked Brachah. They did, and Brachah left Poland with the name and address of a mission school in Paris.

The mission is a secretive institution and does not normally devulge such information, but Brachah, wearing her nun's garb and bearing the passport of Barbara Sokolsky, a missionary from the Holy Land, inspired their confidence.

In her seminary years, Brachah had learned to speak French, and now she reaped the profits of her education. She was as at home in Paris as she had been in Poland. Nor did she have any trouble locating the school. As a nun, the gates of all missions were open to her. Brachah walked into the office and asked for Silvana Borovsky.

"In half an hour," the secretary told her, "Silvana will have a break. You can wait for her in the teacher's room."

The secretary showed Brachah into an empty room, which contained a single long table with many chairs on either side. Brachah sat down and waited. When the teachers started coming into the room, Brachah stood up and walked over to the window opposite the doorway, looking hard at each nun who entered.

Silvana finally came in. Brachah recognized her at once. She smiled warmly and walked toward her. Without a word she stood opposite Silvana, smiling, waiting to be recognized. Silvana stared at Brachah for a minute or two. Then her eyes lit up. "Barbara!" she cried.

Brachah hugged Silvana warmly. "Well, you finally recognized me!"

"Barbara, what are you doing here? Where have you come from? Where have you been all these years?"

Brachah smiled. "You are not giving me a chance to answer you. How can I remember so many questions? Even if I do remember, the answers take more time than the few minutes you have now. Come to my hotel after work today, and then we can talk with no interruptions."

As she spoke, Brachah nodded toward the table where the other teachers sat chatting, hinting that this room was not a suitable place for them to speak freely. She gave Silvana her hotel address and room number and promised to wait for her that afternoon. Then she said good-bye and left. In the yard Brachah watched the schoolgirls playing outside. She saw many Jewish faces and many Jewish eyes, and her heart was heavy.

While she was looking for Sarah in Poland, Brachah had lived on bread and fruit. Now that she was in Paris she could buy a hot meal at a kosher restaurant. Nevertheless, Brachah stuck to a simple diet. She had very little money left and it had to last her. After lunch, she returned to her hotel and went up to her room to wait for Sarah. She had two more hours—enough time for a nap. As soon as Brachah lay down on the sofa she fell asleep. The Angel of Dreams spread his wings over her and brought her father and mother to her in a dream.

Her father Yudel and her mother Esther stood before her, beaming with joy. "How wonderful, Brachah, that you came back to us," said her father.

"I expected this all along. My hopes were not in vain," her mother told her father.

"It is not enough that Brachah has returned. She must bring Sarah back, too," said her father.

"Why, this is the very purpose of her trip," explained her mother.

Suddenly, someone knocked at the door, frightening her father and mother away. Brachah reached out to catch her mother's hand and beg her not to go, but instead her hand hit the wall and she woke up. Someone *was* knocking on the door. It was Sarah. Brachah invited her in and they sat down at the table and began to speak in Polish.

"Where should we start?" asked Brachah.

"You know better than I," smiled Silvana. "I came to hear you tell me your story."

"Well, then," said Brachah, "we will begin not with words but with pictures."

She took a picture out of her wallet and handed it to Sarah. Sarah looked at it and turned white. She dropped the photograph on the table and pushed it away from her.

"Is that the way a daughter treats a picture of her father and mother?" asked Brachah.

"They are no longer my parents . . . they are Jews!"

"Don't say 'they are Jews.' Say 'they *were* Jews' before they were murdered by the Christians."

Shaken, Sarah objected. "It was not Christians who killed the Jews. It was the Nazis."

"All right, let's say it was the Nazis with Christian support. The Poles aided and abetted the Germans in the name of the Church's traditional hatred of the Jews."

"But the Church teaches mercy!"

"That is in theory, but not in practice."

"I don't understand you, Barbara. You are talking like a Jew, not like a Christian."

Brachah ignored Sarah's comment and took another picture from her wallet.

Sarah looked at the picture and exclaimed, "Oh! That's Zushka Yosefova!"

Brachah laughed and said, "No, it's not Zushka Yosefova. It's Zissel Blitz."

Sarah held the picture to her heart and asked, "Where is she now?"

"Zissel is in the Holy Land. I, too, have come from there."

"What brought you to France?"

"I came to show you Zissel's picture. She wants to see you very badly. It would be an act of Christian charity for you to visit her." Brachah pronounced the words 'Christian charity' in a mocking tone.

Stung by her sarcasm, Sarah paused for a minute, and then replied, "You speak as if you have returned to the Jews."

"Don't say 'returned to the Jews.' Say I have returned to myself."

"But you were even more devout a Christian than I! How could you return to the Jews?"

"That's just the point. Let me be your example. If I, who was such a firm believer, could return to my people, it should be much easier for you, who are not so devout."

Sarah did not answer. Brachah too was silent. She must now give Sarah time to absorb all her comments and to argue with herself. For a long time Sarah sat there, motionless, as if in another world. Brachah watched her from the corner of her eye, fully understanding what Sarah was feeling. Finally, Sarah burst into tears, sobbing so hard that her whole body shook.

Brachah went up to her, stroked her head and comforted her. "It is not an easy job to break the bonds that our captors forced upon us while we were at their mercy. It was not easy for me nor is it easy for you. But no one should try to be what he is not. You are a Jew, not a Christian. You were made into a Christian against your will, but you need not stay that way."

For hours the two friends sat and talked. The next day they made reservations on a ship bound for Israel. Many ships left France for Israel, and any Jew who came and asked was given free passage. Sarah did not go to say good-bye to her friends in the mission school. She simply disappeared, just as Brachah had disappeared from the convent in Jerusalem.

Brachah sent a telegram to Zissel, announcing that she and Sarah were setting sail. When the telegram reached the Sharfsons, they found it hard to believe the good news. They read the cable over and over again. Their hearts overflowed with happiness. It was hard to wait two whole weeks. With each day that passed, they became tenser and more excited. It was almost too much to bear.

Finally the day came. The Sharfsons verified the time of the ship's arrival and they all went to Haifa to meet the boat. As they watched the ship cast anchor and saw the gangplank come down, it seemed to them that the beating of their hearts could be heard by everyone in the port.

Finally Sarah appeared. Zissel recognized her immediately and ran to her with outstretched arms. Sarah saw her and opened her arms in response. For what seemed an eternity, the two women stood there, holding each other in a tight embrace. The last of the family had completed her long journey home.

✱ 26 ✱ *Epilogue: The Chasidovs in Eretz Yisrael*

The Sharfson household looked as if it were having a holiday. Accepting Zissel's and Sarah's invitation, the Chasidov families from Nachrovah and Temyonovah had just arrived in Eretz Yisrael. Sarah and Zissel had invited them as a modest expression of thanks for all they had done. They would be honored with trees planted in their names in the Forest of Righteous Gentiles.

There were only four members left in the Chasidov family now. The only son of the Chasidovs of Chedalonova had fought with the Polish partisans and fallen in Yanovsky forest. He himself had not excelled in love for the Jews, but his parents had proved by their deeds that they, at least, were among "the righteous of the nations."

David and Chaim rented a car and took them sightseeing. When they returned to the Sharfsons' house, they were full of praise for all they had seen.

"If we hadn't seen it with our own eyes, we would never have believed it!" they exclaimed enthusiastically.

"No one who knew the Jews of the ghetto could have imagined that they would be capable of building a state like this. Although I have now seen it with my own eyes, it is still hard for me to believe that the Jews did all this by themselves.

"I didn't even recognize the Jews here. In the ghetto all the Jews looked as though they were born bent over and could never stand up straight, but here Jews stand upright. Their eyes are also not the same. The eyes of the Jews in Nachrovah were full of unending sadness, indelible as the color of their eyes. But here I have seen happy eyes. In short, the Jews here are different," said Mr. Chasidov of Nachrovah.

"No," disagreed Mr. Chasidov of Chedalonova, "they are the same Jews. Their troubles in Chedalonova and Nachrovah made them different."

There are new faces in the Sharfson house today. Not only are Brachah and David married; Sarah and Chaim have also found their life's partners. Three new Jewish families have been founded. Now they are all assembled in the Sharfson house, awaiting the return of Rav Shlomo Sharfson from the *yeshivah*. When he comes, they will all sit down to a festive meal with their honored guests.

Later that afternoon, they all went to the forest. The Chasidov brothers and their wives each stood bent over his or her sapling, covering it firmly with the warm earth. The Sharfson and Glick families stood to the side, watching them admiringly. When the Chasidovs finished, their eyes were filled with tears. They were deeply moved. Almost automatically, all eyes turned to Shlomo, to hear what he would say to the guests on this occasion.

Shlomo turned to them and began. "The people of Israel have a long history. Over three thousand six hundred years have passed since the first Jew was born. A nation that old should number billions of souls, yet there are only a few million Jews alive in the world today. Throughout the centuries, other nations have cut off whole branches of the Jewish race. Even Abraham, the first Jew, was himself thrown into a burning furnace. Anyone who smashes idols is bound to be hated by idol-worshipers.

"At Mount Sinai the people of Israel became the symbol of belief in one God. As recipients of the Ten Commandments, they became, at the same time, the object of an eternal hatred by all other nations. The rest of the world can never forgive the Jews for the message of the Ten Commandments which they brought to the world—a message to restrain Man's baser instincts. All those who desire to give free rein to their baser instincts must of necessity become the enemies of Israel.

"This forest was planted by righteous Gentiles. Look around and see how few trees have been planted here, and you will realize how universal anti-Semitism is. The world numbers billions of human beings, but very few righteous people. Their small number emphasizes their exceptional courage.

"If, in the vast sea of anti-Semitism, there are still a few scattered Gentiles who are willing to endanger their own lives to save the lives of Jews, there can be no greater spiritual courage than this. These few deserve our unbounded admiration and recognition."

Shlomo paused. The Chasidovs' eyes were lowered modestly.

"After all the world has done to the Jewish People," he

continued, "there are still Jews alive the world over, and they are gradually returning to the land that God promised our forefathers. This is nothing less than a miracle. God does not perform miracles for no reason. This miracle is the strongest possible proof that the God of Israel is true to His people. The nation of Israel is eternal; it will outlast all the wicked of the other nations. This is the source of our strength. This is the belief that has enabled us to bear such a heavy burden for so many centuries."

Shlomo paused again and then concluded, " 'I believe with perfect faith in the coming of the *Mashiach*. And even though he tarries, I will wait for him, day after day, until he comes.' "

another novel by
BENZION FIRER

The Twins

As the brutalities of World War II tore mercilessly through the towns and cities of Poland, helpless Jewish communities by the thousands were ravaged and left in ruins and misery.

When Yudel and Esther Glick were forced into the ghetto of Nachrovah, they knew how black the situation was. They did not delude themselves. And yet they did not give up in despair. It became their determination to keep the light of the Torah burning brightly in the dark night of the ghetto; and when death had to be faced, they went on willingly, as Heaven's martyrs, *al kiddush haShem*.

Their twin children, Chaim and Brachah, remain alive through everything, but in all the chaos and confusion of the war, they become separated. Years of turbulence and upheaval pass. Yet even over great stretches of time and space, there are bonds of the spirit within them that cannot be cut, and eventually the two are united despite all the difficulties they have lived through.

In this unusual, poignant story that vividly portrays a period of Jewish suffering and despair in our time, the central characters of the novel journey with heart-warming courage and faith across a landscape of death and destruction, to find, eventually, new shelter and new hope in the Land of Israel.

Translated by Bracha Slae

another novel by
BENZION FIRER

Saadiah Weissman

In the first hectic years after the declaration of the State of Israel, as waves of Jewish immigrants converged from east to west upon the tiny, struggling country, great deeds and great tragedies took place side by side.

When thousands of Jews—God-fearing people all—arrived from Yemen on "wings of eagles" as promised by the prophets of old, each was ready to greet the *mashiach* in the Holy Land of Israel. But instead of the *mashiach*, they found the 20th century—a strange, bewildering world which left them vulnerable and disoriented.

One of the most disturbing aspects of those tumultuous years was the unaccountable disappearance of hundreds of Yemenite children who had arrived in Israel only to vanish from the face of the earth. Persistent rumors had it that they were given away for adoption to non-religious Israeli families or sent to non-religious kibbutzim. Saadiah Weissman is the story of one such child—one child and two families whose lives, although vastly different, were tragically intermingled.

This absorbing novel, with its nearly disastrous ending, cannot fail to move the reader as it portrays the period from Israel's founding through the next two decades.

Translated by Chava Shulman